SLIPBACK

DOCTOR WHO

SLIPBACK

ERIC SAWARD

Based on the BBC radio serial by Eric Saward by arrangement with the British Broadcasting Corporation

---

TARGET

A TARGET BOOK

published by
the Paperback Division of
W.H. ALLEN & CO PLC

A Target Book
Published in 1987
By the Paperback Division of
W.H. Allen & Co. PLC
44 Hill Street, London W1X 8LB

First published in Great Britain by
W.H. Allen & Co. PLC 1986

Typeset in Baskerville by Fleet Graphics, Enfield, Middlesex

Printed and bound in Great Britain by
Anchor Brendon Ltd, Tiptree, Essex

ISBN0 426 20263 5

CONTENTS

For Jane,
with fondest love

PART ONE
In the Beginning . . .

1

The *Vipod Mor*

The galaxy of Setna Streen was not unlike our own so-called Milky Way. At its centre, a mass of stars seemed to form a flat dice or hub. Spiralling out from this were what appeared to be 'S'-shaped spokes that tapered into thin mists. In fact, the whole thing, when viewed from afar, looked very much like a Catherine wheel frozen in all its glory.

The more romantic preferred to see it as another sort of wheel, its rim now broken and decayed, but one that was once part of a chariot that carried some long-forgotten god across the heavens. As most galaxies are of a similar shape, cynics were heard to echo that this mobile deity was a rather reckless and messy driver. Not only did he appear to break a great many wheels, but he was very casual in the way he abandoned his debris all over the universe.

Now, it is interesting to note that towards the end of the twentieth century, a man from Earth, by the name of Horace Noakes, set out to prove that the 'chariot wheel' theory was true.

Of course people laughed, especially as he cited the so-called myths put about by the ancient Greeks. Horace reasoned that these were not stories inspired by a surfeit of *retsina* or *ouzo*, but genuine sightings.

When the scientific establishment had stopped sneering, they started to examine his evidence more closely, hoping that it would provide them with a few more smirks and sniggers.

In his book *The Giants Who Walked the Heavens - An Everyday Story of Cosmos Folk*, Horace went on to argue the significance of the Zodiac signs.

As we now know, the various group of stars we call constellations are not related in any way at all. In fact, many of the stars making up such a cluster are often separated by hundreds of light years. It is only the perspective placed on them, when viewed from Earth, that gives them any form of tenuous relationship. This, of course, is known by any three-year old with an IQ of minus ten. The real puzzle was why those particular stars had been chosen to make up the configuration imposed upon them, when it was obvious to a dead Voltrox that they didn't resemble the image they were supposed to represent.

Horace had an answer for this.

He reckoned that the ancient Greeks knew that these stars were vast distances apart and that the various clusters were never meant to represent the named images they were given, but were simply reference points to establish the size and shape of a living person or creature they had seen in the heavens.

The howls of hysterical laughter from the scientific establishment grew louder and coarser.

In an attempt to create some sort of credibility, Horace set about proving mathematically that the proportions of his heavenly giants were on the same scale as the spiral galaxies, and that such enormous people required wheels of similar dimension for their carts and chariots.

This was too much for the scientists. Sick with laughter, they took out their pocket calculators and started to prod and jab at them, in the laid-back way mathematicians do, pausing only to crack subtle, academic jokes such as: 'I'd've hated to clear up after a horse the size necessary to pull such a chariot!'

But as the digital answers flashed up on their digital screens, they paused and wiped the tears of laughter from their faces. Horace's calculations *seemed* to be correct. 'It wasn't possible!' they cried as one voice. And not wanting to appear any more foolish than they were, they immediately set about trying to find other ways to discredit him.

But they could have saved their effort as they had already succeeded in planting the seeds of ridicule in people's minds.

When Horace's book was finally published, it was viciously attacked by the critics. This was sad, as no-one had been able to disprove anything he had written. It was even sadder that the critics, blinded by their own prejudice, could not see the energy, grace and skill that had gone into the book's construction. Even if, as they believed, every word was untrue, they chose to ignore the incredible flights of imagination necessary to argue such a theory. But worse still – as they were supposedly people of education and letters – they could not see or appreciate the pure, good writing which was on the page.

Although the book sold well, it was bought for all the wrong reasons. People would memorise passages from it, then regurgitate them at drinks parties, laughing like blocked drains as they did. It had become chic to mock Horace.

Unable to cope with the ridicule, Horace retired into obscurity. Two years later he died of a broken heart.

While Horace had been suffering his terrible torment, a scholar by the name of Grigory Constintine had been working on deciphering a language known as Linear A. Now, so-called Linear A was the written language used by the ancient Greeks. Although scholars had spent a great deal of time attempting to interpret the script, it had remained elusive. That was until Grigory had discovered the key.

Possessive of his new-found knowledge (and concerned that he might be mistaken), Grigory would not allow anyone in on his secret until he was satisfied that he could decipher any random Linear A inscription.

Locked in a small room at the Athens museum, he worked

on the many clay tablets which had been discovered on archaeological digs all over Greece. But the more he studied, the more he became withdrawn, until people began to believe Grigory had been mistaken, and that he had not been able to decipher the script.

Then one day he announced that he was to publish his findings. Unfortunately, Grigory showed the only copy of his manuscript to a colleague. Later that evening his work room was broken into and the manuscript along with several vital clay tablets were stolen.

Neither thief, manuscript nor tablets were ever found. Grigory was convinced this was because the scientific establishment never wanted it, for the missing tablets confirmed Horace Noakes's theory to the last detail.

Of course, no-one believed Grigory and dismissed his claims as some sort of publicity stunt, which was considered to be in rather bad taste for a man of his brilliance and academic standing.

Like Horace, Grigory died a broken man, even though he went down in history as the person who had deciphered Linear A. The year was 1996 AD.

Now, although Setna Streen was not unlike our own galaxy in shape, there were many major differences. Whereas the Milky Way can only boast of two planets inhabited by intelligent life forms, Setna has seventeen.

Why Setna proved more conducive to the production of life was a bit of a mystery, as was the fact that the life forms evolved much faster than those in the Milky Way. Some anthropologists have put this development down to the cultivation of the grape.

On Earth, so-called *homo sapiens* in his early stage of development seemed happy enough to live in caves, hunt mammoths, dress himself in skins and win the company of a spouse by killing her relatives and then carrying her off to his part of the swamp.

In Setna Streen it was very different. Long before any

12

member of the galaxy had even learnt the art of making fire, they discovered the joy of over-ripe grapes fermenting on the vine.

Such was the pleasure derived from eating such fruit that they wanted to experience this delectation all year round. But vines, even in Setna, only produce one crop a year. Therefore it was necessary to find ways to store the grapes.

To achieve this, they first had to invent the barrel. Once this had been done, they soon learnt that only the juice of the grape was necessary to produce what became known as wine.

But drinking from a barrel was not only difficult, but wasteful, as it was inclined to be spilt. It was then necessary to invent glass. Not only was it more pleasant to drink out of a leaded crystal goblet, they also found that wine kept very well in bottles.

Now, as any good vintner knows, cork is still the most effective way to seal a bottle, which meant they had to learn how to smelt iron so that they could invent the corkscrew.

As we all know, the production of wine also attracts the people from Customs and Excise, who, somehow, along the way, had managed to invent themselves. Now, why the people from C and E should be so interested in wine is still a mystery, for all they want is to tax it, not enjoy the pleasure of its consumption. So it then became necessary for the population of Setna to invent ships and aeroplanes so that they could justify the duty free shop.

And so it went on.

It is interesting to note that when the joy of wine was discovered on Earth, massive, wonderfully creative civilisation soon followed – Egypt, Greece, Rome. When these empires crumbled, and wine became a scarce commodity, civilisation sank into the Dark Ages. It wasn't until wine once more became plentiful that surges of energy known as the Renaissance occurred. Fortunately, during one of these periods of creativity, the off-licence was invented, and since then the people of Earth have never looked back.

The other inhabited planet of the Milky Way, Snibbits 9, never did invent wine. So, until this day its people still live in caves and commune closely with nature. In some parts of the universe, this planet is known as Paradise; in others as Hell.

When the history of the universe is finally written, it will be seen that wine was the greatest single factor in promoting both artistic and technological evolution.

Although Setna had had its fair share of both domestic and interplanetary wars, it had also enjoyed periods of harmonious peace, as, in fact, it was doing now. Whenever one of these lulls occurred the interplanetary council would meet and try and decide how best to exploit the peace.

Inevitably, the word *tourism* would creep into the conversation.

Now as a rule, tourism usually assists peace. After all, there is nothing better for curing racial prejudice than to pack a bucket, spade and flip-flops and spend a fortnight visiting *foreigners* in their own lair. Usually it takes no more than a couple of days to unwind before you become aware of how pleasant and agreeable the natives are. By the end of the first week you have learnt that, apart from the language, you aren't that different from each other after all. By the end of the second week you don't really want to go home. When you finally do, you then spend the long winter months pining over a collection of out of focus holiday snaps and saving to go back, or to somewhere even more foreign.

Only fools say that travel doesn't broaden the mind. It's true that it is very difficult to develop any major insight into another nation when all you do while there is spend your time activating the melanin in your skin by lying on the beach. But simply *being* in a foreign land does slowly develop empathy, while at the same time whittling down to size our own national arrogance.

The same would have been true for the people of Setna if only they had allowed themselves to get on with their holidays. But the authorities wouldn't allow them to.

Each planet felt that it had more to offer than any of the others, and therefore wanted to be the centre of all tourist activities. Unfortunately, such silly selfishness had led to several interplanetary wars.

It wasn't until someone suggested that an independent committee be set up to study the tourist possibilities of each planet that any progress was made. Wisely, the committee decided to ignore all 'official' information supplied in favour of their own separate survey.

When announcing their intention, the committee had expected resistance from the various governments. However, instead, they became very excited and suggested the project be expanded to include a thorough archaeological and anthropological study of each planet too.

So instead of hiring a freighter, as had been the original plan, money was found to build a proper survey ship, which was to include all the necessary facilities vital to such a mission

It took five years to construct the craft and, when finished it was the finest of its kind. As a token of good will, it was painted green, the Setna colour for peace.

Now all the ship lacked was a name.

At first this proved difficult, as each planet wanted one which reflected its own particular endeavour and commitment to the project. It wasn't until someone suggested the name *Vipod Mor* that the problem was solved.

The story concerning Vipod Mor is interesting only in as much as he was an enigma. He only ever made one appearance, but such was its technological brilliance that it has never been forgotten.

About five hundred years ago, when the planets of Setna were busy putting up artificial satellites, sending out deep space probes and generally showing off by putting people on their respective moons, an old man, looking very much like an Old Testament prophet, came amongst them. He said that his name was Vipod Mor, that he was a Time Lord, and that his mission was to warn the people of Setna against the dangers of experimenting with time-travel.

Now this seemed rather strange advice, given that technologically the people of Setna were as far away from time experiments as the inventor of the wheel was from being able to build a motor car. This made the people of Setna wonder whether the old boy had simply got the wrong galaxy, or that the whole thing was a massive hoax.

Neither did it help to clarify the confusion with the method he had used to announce his message. Unlike the prophets of the past, who would drift into town, make their way to the market square, rent a soap box and deliver their message of doom or salvation to a bemused crowd, he had used television.

But not in the conventional way. That would have been too simple. Instead he had somehow managed to cut into the regular transmission of every television company on each and every planet of Setna Streen.

To have achieved such a take-over on just one planet would have been, for those days, a brilliant technological feat. But simultaneously on all seventeen was a near miracle.

Of course the various planets didn't know that at the time. It wasn't until a hundred and fifty years later, when the warp engine had been perfected, and interplanetary travel was possible, that the people of Setna learned the truth.

Yet the mystery remained. Why had Vipod Mor gone to all that trouble? And why had he made his declaration so long before anyone in Setna had the technical skills necessary for time travel?

The crew of the survey ship *Vipod Mor*, much to their distress, would find out why.

2

The Life and Times of
Shellingborne Grant

Running at quarter speed, the *Vipod Mor* coasted gently through space. Something was wrong with one of the main warp engines. Although the onboard computer searched frantically for the fault, she was unable to locate the precise problem.

The crew twiddled their thumbs and waited. Waiting was something they weren't used to.

The ship was now into the eighth year of its ten year mission to survey all the planets of Setna Streen. Up until a week ago the ship had functioned perfectly, requiring nothing more than routine maintenance. Now everything seemed to be going wrong: niggling things that took hours to repair.

Even the onboard computer had become a little scatty. She would often forget or confuse her instructions, offering false or irrelevant data.

It seemed as though everything aboard the ship was wearing out at the same time. The Chief Engineer had assured the Captain that this was impossible. Even if the computer failed to report a malfunction, the rigorous maintenance programme operated by his repair team would pick up most faults before they became critical. The poor man was still arguing his case when a deck plate gave way beneath him. Such was his terrible cursing, as he tumbled

17

through the black void, into the service ducting below, that it caused a heavy duty steam pipe to rupture and he was scalded to death.

Needless to say, this incident did not help to reassure the Captain as to the worthiness of his ship, especially as the offending deck plate was in his cabin.

Neither was the ship's morale improved when the party sent to retrieve the Chief's body reported that all they could find were his boots.

At first, the Captain thought that the Chief was still alive, and, because of his confused or concussed state, had simply wandered off into the endless service shafts.

But when the search party found the remains of a fresh, human femur, there was little doubt what had happened: the Chief Engineer had been eaten by something rather unpleasant.

Immediately the computer was set to work to locate the intruder, while further search parties, under the direction of Second Lieutenant Shellingborne Grant, were sent to investigate the areas of the ducting beyond the computer's scrutiny.

Grant, who was the *Vipod Mor*'s so-called computer expert, wasn't pleased with his current task. He had never liked the Chief Engineer, finding him a bullish, pedantic individual, who seemed to have more rapport with the machines he serviced than with other members of the crew. At least that is what he told people at cocktail parties.

The real reason was somewhat more calculated and mercenary.

Although only thirty-five years old, Shellingborne Grant had led a very full life. His natural good looks and superficial, easy-going personality made him very agreeable company. But Grant wasn't an honest person. In fact, he was quite the reverse with an almost pathological hatred of being poor.

Of course, there is no virtue in being poor. Anyone who

has tried to secure a small loan from a bank, without collateral, is only too aware of how managers of such establishments view those sort of requests. To be able to borrow money requires that you already have some, in one form or another, which somehow seems to make the loan side of banking rather redundant.

But Grant was never *poor*-poor. He always had enough to eat, somewhere warm and moderately comfortable to live and rarely went without what passed for fashionable clothing.

Yet when asked why he wanted to be rich, he could never offer a positive answer. He certainly didn't have any ambition to own a large house in one of the fashionable areas of his planet. Neither did he want his own space shuttle with or without tinted glass, speelsnape skin-covered seats and polished alloy exhaust ports.

He just wanted to be *rich* and have a fifteen figure bank account.

On hearing this, his friends thought that Grant had hidden vices which required vast amounts of cash to be indulged. But they were mistaken as Grant had told the truth for once in his life: *he just wanted to be rich.*

Achieving this was something else. The easiest way was to be born into a wealthy family. The best way was to inherit it without any complicated ties. The least agreeable, although still acceptable in criminal circles, was to marry a gullible, wealthy widow. Another way, of course, was to be become an 'expert' in some arcane subject that has cash value to industry. But this required talent, dedication *and* hard work, something Grant was allergic to. It also required an excellent brain to be a genius, which Grant also didn't have. The only academic pennant he could fly was a second class honours degree in computer design and shoe repairing. (A second subject was mandatory at the university he attended. Most students chose something which complemented their main one – but not Grant.)

Yet, being a computer designer did give him access to the machines where other people's money, ideas and secrets were stored. This he decided to exploit and a year later he was arrested for embezzlement. Fortunately for him, but unfortunately for society, he was let out on bail, which he promptly jumped. He then stowed away on board a space freighter destined for Praxis 30, a remote planet on the edge of Setna Streen. At the age of twenty-two he had granted himself the honour of becoming an interplanetary crook.

And so it went on.

Although Grant was able to buy another identity, with the chance of building a new life, he always spoilt things by stealing from those who trusted him.

By the time he was twenty-six he was wanted for embezzlement on twelve separate planets. All of a sudden the galaxy was becoming too small for him.

Then one night, while drinking in a Voxnic bar on Zaurak Minor – considered by some to be the seediest planet in the galaxy – Grant met, or rather fell over a disbarred brain surgeon by the name of Oliver Sneed.

In his day, Sneed had been considered the greatest specialist in his subject, that was until someone discovered how specialised he had become. Sneed, apart from being a brilliant surgeon, was also a great gambler, prepared to bet on almost anything, especially when drunk. For some unknown reason he believed that his 'luck' was inviolable when he was inebriated. It was true that he had been very fortunate in the past, making the most outrageous bets and winning. But never before had he gambled with his reputation. It was to prove his undoing.

The event occurred one dark, wet evening when Sneed was guest of honour at the Interplanetary Psychologists and Psychiatrists Convention. It always seemed to rain when the psychs were in town. No-one seemed to know why. As soon as such a convention was announced heavy, dark cúmulus-nimbus clouds would gather over the building designated as

20

the venue. Usually it would start raining about a week before they arrived, the downpour becoming even heavier whilst the conference was in session. Yet as soon as it was over, out would pop the sun. If the psychs had decided to become rain dancers, rather than brain experts, they would have made a fortune.

Legend has it that the people of Morbus, a planet noted for its convention facilities, grew tired of the deluge which accompanied their gatherings. Yet as their business was hosting conventions, they felt they couldn't let such valuable customers down. After all, it wasn't the psychs' fault it always rained when they gathered *en masse,* but at the same time the people of Morbus were looking forward to a pleasant summer.

After much discussion starships were sent out to search the nearby galaxy for another planet which could provide a suitable venue. The starships travelled far and wide until they came across a pretty, blue planet inhabited by simple folk who spent their days having a good time.

Not wanting to exploit the local people, the representatives from Morbus shopped around until they found a farmer who would rent them a few hectacres of land for the period of time required. On making the deal, they quickly erected a temporary convention centre and then warned the farmer of the impending rain storm, suggesting he took necessary precautions. Thinking he would go away and invent the umbrella or plastic raincoat or something similar, they went home.

But the farmer over-reacted, concerned by what a downpour could do to his corner of the desert. So, after a lot of consideration, he invented the container ship and loaded onto it everything he thought might prove useful.

In due course the delegates arrived and, as predicted, it started to rain as it had never rained before. Unfortunately several knotty problems arose which caused the convention to over-run its allotted fortnight by nearly four weeks.

So heavy had been the rain that when they finally emerged from the conference, they found they were surrounded by an ocean.

As the delegates boarded their starship, the flight computer informed them that its sensors had just picked up the presence of a small, drifting vessel. Further investigation showed it was the ship built by the farmer. On its bow was emblased the name *SS Ark*. It is interesting to note how the intrusion of alien life-forms can affect not only the ecology of a planet but also its history and myths.

After Sneed had delivered his highly controversial speech to the convention – *The Advantages of Psycho-Surgery Over Both Chemo and Long Term Deep Analysis* – he sat back and waited for his audience to explode.

Now, it should be understood that psychiatrists and their camp followers are very touchy when it comes to having their methods criticised. Why this should be a complaint common to all psychs is yet another great mystery. Paranoia is the most common psychiatric condition known, yet it is most prevalent in the profession committed to understanding and eradicating it.

Setna was not an exception. In that particular galaxy, like elsewhere, there are two schools of thought concerning the treatment of mentally disturbed patients. The cheapest, and therefore the most common, is the use of drugs to stabilise what is believed to be a chemical imbalance in the brain. Whether mental disorder has anything to do with chemicals, or anything else, has yet to be proved, although drug therapy does make the patient calmer. Of course the success of such treatment is very much down to the prescribing doctor, who must get the prescription absolutely right if the patient is to make any form of recovery.

There are many critics of this method who argue that you are simply treating the symptoms of the condition and not the cause. These critics, needless to say, belong mainly to the second school of psychiatric thought.

They call themselves psychoanalysts.

In brief, they believe that 'life' - ie. people - screw each other up. Why your own species should have this effect on itself is the greatest mystery of all. But, indisputably, it does.

Therefore it is vital that the patient comes to terms with 'life', and its accompanying feelings of frustration and inadequacy, by examining their problems and ultimately coming to understand them.

This is much easier said than done, as treatment is always very painful. After all, who wants to meet, let alone come to terms with, one's *real* self, as such a festering tangle can never be a pretty sight. What's more, the patients are expected to unravel this mess for themselves, ironing out the twisted strands until they take on a shape and proportion resembling normality.

This process of self-examination - hopefully developing self-understanding - is supposed to lead to a healthy state of chemistry in the brain. In other words, same ends, as the chemo-therapists, but very different means.

But unlike drug treatment, the *cause* is also supposed to be dealt with and not just the symptoms.

This analysis, as it is called, is usually done under the strict supervision of a psychiatrist. As the treatment is often very lengthy, it is also very expensive. Therefore to receive such treatment you either have to be very rich *or very mad*.

Now, there is only one subject that both schools of psychiatric thought agreed upon, and that was in their attitude towards the ideas promulgated by Sneed. To operate on the brain for the purpose of supposedly curing a personality disorder, or a psychosis or neurosis, was an anathema to them. After all, they would have argued, you don't cut a person's nose off simply because they have a cold.

Their attitude stems from the days when psycho-surgery was used to 'restore' a state of conscience to otherwise disruptive members of society. These people were called sociopaths and the surgical technique used to 'stabilise' them was called a lobotomy.

This involved chopping about the frontal lobe of the brain, in a controlled manner, which was then supposed to make the patient a happy, more agreeable person.

In reality it was far less successful, often altering the personality of the lobotomised subjects to such an extent that they were almost unrecognisable. Instead of a happy, useful person who could then go on to contribute, rather than destroy, the operation often reduced them to smiling imbeciles.

To be fair, it must be understood that the reason for the failure of these early experiments in psycho-surgery was due mainly to not understanding how the brain functioned. Things have since changed.

Of course, the techniques used by Sneed were much more sophisticated, and as his experiments on animals had shown, they were completely successful – that is, in as far as they went.

But as always, Oliver had over-stated his case. He made all sorts of claims for techniques that were untried and untested. He also boasted that he could raise the IQ of a congenital idiot, using psycho-surgery, to well above average intelligence.

His audience was outraged, which pleased Sneed no end. But he had gone too far. He had forgotten that he was addressing a convention of *professional* psychiatrists and psychologists. Although the distinguished gathering may not have possessed Sneed's intimate knowledge of psycho-surgery, they were all very well read, and knew precisely the level to which the techniques had been perfected. The sad thing was that Oliver had not considered this simple fact, his intake of Voxnic having fuddled his otherwise sharp mind.

But on the other hand, he had never *expected* to be taken seriously. He had just wanted to be controversial and stir up an otherwise dull convention. Yet right up until the last

24

moment he could have reneged on his assertions, admitted that it was 'all a bit of fun.'

But he didn't.

After listening to Oliver's exaggerated claims, the audience had settled down, more in stunned silence than for any other reason. The Chairperson, desperate to conclude Oliver's session, switched on a formal smile and started to deliver his usual finishing speech: 'If there are no further questions, I would like to thank – ' The remainder of the sentence was lost in uproar from the audience. *Finished*! They hadn't even started. Before Oliver left the podium, they wanted to see the skin flailed from his argument, the soft parts of its body cut off with a rusty, blunt knife and fed to a pack of razor-billed voltroxes.

Oliver took a large gulp from his glass of Voxnic. Foolishly, he was still enjoying himself.

As the audience came to order, a soft voice was heard to echo from the back of the hall. Oliver leant forward to catch what was being said. He had learned from his days as a lecturer that the *soft*-voiced students often gave him the most trouble.

He was not to be disappointed.

The voice wanted to know why Oliver had not published his research concerning this surgical technique for improving intelligence. *Because I haven't done any!* he shouted inside his head. But out loud he was more expedient: 'Because it would prove too controversial . . . ' He paused for dramatic effect. 'As, I might add, your reaction has proven.' He smiled smugly to himself, pleased with his reply.

'So you prefer,' the soft voice was now insistent, 'to appear a fool by making outrageous and unsubstantiated statements?'

A deathly hush settled over the hall. Soft Voice was out for blood. They could sense it. And there was nothing more such a convention enjoyed than to see a pre-eminent specialist on the run.

'You're right,' said Oliver slowly, finally realising he had left it too late to withdraw. 'Although I wouldn't have phrased it quite as you have.' But the audience didn't titter or smile as he had hoped. They weren't going to let him off.

Oliver slurped another mouthful of Voxnic. He was now playing for time as he knew that his answer had to be a good one.

Of course, he could try making a fuss along the lines of *I've never been so insulted in all my life*, but he knew he had gone too far and left it too late for that. If he became outraged he would lose what was left of his credibility. And that was the last thing he wanted. The medical fraternity is claustrophobically small, making it very difficult to manoeuvre if you were considered unreliable. Oliver knew this and had to counteract it at once. Somehow he must prove that he was touched by genius.

But it was all too late.

Suddenly the gulp of Voxnic hit his stomach. He felt inspired. He would show them that he *was* a genius. His gambler's instinct had never failed him before, and now he felt supremely confident.

'You're absolutely right,' he repeated, steadying himself on the lectern before him. 'I shall do more than publish my notes.' He looked confidently around the hall. 'By the time this conference reconvenes next year, I shall not only have published my researches, but also provide you with living proof of them!' The hall gasped.

And so they should. Out loud he said 'What's more, I shan't bother with a mere human, but will raise, using psycho-surgery, an animal . . . ' He thought for a second. 'I shall provide you with a speelsnape,' he continued, 'which has all the mental attributes of a living human being.'

The hall bustled with excited chatter. Although the Chair-person worked his gabble up and down with the speed of a racing piston in a runaway engine, he was unable to obtain order.

As Oliver left the conference hall, he was as high as a morphine addict. *Top that*! was his attitude. But none of his critics could. Come to that, neither could he.

Oliver retired to his laboratory and immediately fell into a deep depression. Why had he chosen a speelsnape? Of all the animals in the galaxy why that one? *Because your mind was fuddled with alcohol* boomed an inner voice. And it was right.

Speelsnapes were not pleasant creatures. Weighing approximately fifty-five kilos, it is a little bigger than a large dog. But there the similarity ends. With the speed of a cheetah, the temperament of a psychopathic crocodile on a bad day, it lives for only two things: to eat, and to reproduce.

Genetically it is indomitable, being able to mate with any creature of roughly its own size. Be the mother pig, dog, sheep or voltrox, its offspring will always be one hundred per cent, undiluted, male speelsnape. The reason for what appears an arbitrary choice of mate is simple. Once the young speelsnape is born, its first meal is its mother. Speelsnapes eat.nothing but meat. Ever.

With teeth as sharp as scalpels and jaw muscles exercising the power of hydraulic jacks, it is able to chew, rip and tear its way through the body of any living thing. Like the wild cat or African elephant, it is completely untameable, prepared,to die rather than be taken. Needless to say, there are very few in captivity.

To its credit, it is a very beautiful animal, with the grace and agility of a cat. Its coat is smooth and sleek, consisting of a fine, downy-like fur which is much prized for seat covers. (Perhaps another reason why it is so difficult to catch?) But because of its tenacity and powerful instinct for survival, many customers have to wait a very long time before they are privileged to boast of the ownership of even one pelt.

Although Oliver worked long and hard, one complex problem after another continued to defeat him. After nine months of mind-numbing work, he was no nearer solving his problems than on the first day.

That was until he was unexpectedly called to hospital to attend a patient recently involved in a space shuttle accident. As Oliver examined the severe cranium fracture, a terrible thought came into his mind. *Why struggle to intellectually raise the speelsnape's brain when all I need do is replace it with a human one!*

And so he did. But although the transfer was totally successful, he was found out. What's more, no one was particularly impressed by what he had achieved and he was thrown out of his profession and barred from practising medicine throughout Setna.

At first, Grant had been bored with Oliver's story, but as it had progressed, an idea almost as terrible as Oliver's own had occurred to him. If he were to avoid capture by the police, he would require a new face, but something much more sophisticated than could be provided by the average back-street plastic surgeon. Even with a change of facial features, there was still the problem of his fingerprints.

But with a new body *all* his problems would be solved!

The more he considered it, the more excited he became. But could he trust Oliver? He only had his word that he was who he said he was. And even if he were Oliver Sneed, did he still possess the skill necessary to transplant his brain into another body?

But what did Grant have to lose? The police weren't far behind and the thought of spending the next fifteen years in prison didn't appeal to him at all. He would take the chance!

And he did.

The operation cost Grant every penny of his not inconsiderable fortune. But that didn't matter as the transplant had been successful! He had no idea where Oliver had found his new body, but then he didn't really want to know. The frame was fit and healthy and that was all that mattered.

The only problem he experienced was coming to terms with the larger bulk of his new shape. He was seven centimetres taller and much more muscular than his old frame.

But as he was also four years younger, Grant felt it made up for the initial inconvenience.

As he had recently purchased the identity of Shellingborne Grant, and as far as he knew the police were unaware of his new name, he decided to keep it, especially as the real Mr Grant had an impeccable history and references.

His next consideration was what he was going to do with himself. He was broke, but worse still, he was a man who was broke who was cursed with very extravagant tastes. It would only be a matter of time before Grant started to look around for yet more money to embezzle. What he needed was a quiet job which would take him out of circulation – and out of the way of temptation – yet at the same time, create for himself a genuine history.

And that was how Grant became the officer in charge of the onboard computer of the *Vipod Mor*. Other and better qualified people had applied for the post, but he was the only one prepared to sign on for the full ten year mission. Grant realised that it was a long time, but he had plenty of that particular commodity. By the time his contract ended, his brain would be thirty-six years old, but his body a mere thirty-two. He would also get the chance to see the whole galaxy, and who could tell what criminal inspiration that would give him.

But Grant didn't have to wait that long.

The *Vipod Mor* was only three days into its maiden flight when its Captain received a message. It had been decided at an extraordinary meeting of the interplanetary governments that a permanent exhibition was to be created to celebrate the planets' unprecedented co-operation. A huge space station would be built and furnished with treasures and works of art representing the finest moments in each planet's history. The space station would then be known as *The Museum of Peace and Understanding*. And to prove the point, the galaxy would also become a Federation of Unified Planets.

Although this was good news, it would also prove to be a

great deal of extra work for the crew of the *Vipod Mor*, as their mission was now expanded to include the transportation of the so-called 'treasures of peace'.

At first, Grant moaned and groaned along with everyone else, until he realised the criminal opportunity with which he was being presented. Instead of going out to steal, the goods were actually being brought to him! As the computer was to be used to catalogue the treasures, and he was in charge of that particular machine, it would require little effort on his part to erase from the catalogue any choice items which took his fancy. All it then required was for him to slip along to the hold and remove the item. By the time the treasures were unpacked, and someone realised that things were missing, he would be long gone.

His only real problem, Grant decided, would be storing his swag. It was then that he approached the Chief Engineer, offering to 'rent' space in an obscure corner of his service ducting. Although the Chief didn't want to know why he had made such a request, he was too honest and too rulebook-bound to agree. It was about this time that Grant had decided he didn't like the Chief Engineer.

Undeterred, Grant consulted the computer, which provided a list of remote areas which were unlikely to be entered by the maintenance teams in the course of the ship's mission.

As Grant checked the suggested areas for suitability, he couldn't help wondering about the comment the computer had made when providing the list: 'I can keep a secret, too, you know.' He was aware that the computer was a highly advanced, complex machine which had been programmed to be 'user-friendly', but nowhere in her programming was she supposed to be 'conspiratorial'.

It worried Grant a little. Perhaps the computer builders had omitted to tell him something. He was aware that the designers were still trying to make sense of some of the features which had been included in her logic circuits, as these complex cells had been designed by other computers. But using computers to build bigger ones wasn't unusual. And on occasions, the experts managed to work out what happened to be *odd* design features. Eventually.

Grant decided to dismiss the incident from his mind. It was something he would live to regret.

3

Something Nasty in the Ducting

Shellingborne Grant sat on the bridge of the *Vipod Mor* and examined his finger nails. He had cut them only the previous day, yet they needed cutting again.

Although Grant had now occupied his new body for eight years, he had never really come to terms with some of its activities. Not only did his nails grow more quickly than those on his old frame but also the hair on both his head and chin. Being lazy when it came to personal hygiene, he still resented having to shave twice a day. Needless to say this wasn't out of choice, but by the Captain's order.

Grant had never understood the Captain's insistence for a 'well turned-out crew'. At first he thought it had something to do with discipline. But what had a well scraped chin or having to wear full uniform on duty have to do with self-motivation or efficiency, he had often asked himself.

That was until he experienced the Captain's first inspection. One by one, over a period of several days, each member of the crew (and there were nearly seven hundred of them) was summoned to his cabin and lectured on the importance of hygiene. To the Captain, bodily hair was a nest of potential evil, places for all sorts of bacteria to hibernate, spawn and grow. If he had had his way, all bodily hair would have been removed.

As early interviewees emerged from the Captain's cabin and related what had been said, waves of fear spread throughout the ship, especially amongst the male members of the crew.

In Setna, it is traditional for men to wear their hair long as an indication of their strength and masculinity. The thought of their well-coiffured locks being shorn instantly caused twenty of them to steal an escape pod and desert.

Concerned that he might lose more of his crew, the Captain considered it expedient to revise his thinking. So instead he ordered that the crew could keep their hair, but insisted it be washed daily, and that beards were to be forbidden. This the crew accepted.

Now it wasn't that the Captain was a pervert, at least not about hair. He believed what he believed because he thought it was right. But younger members of the crew did find it rather disconcerting when they discovered him lurking in gangways in the middle of the night, demanding to check the growth on their chins. Even the excuse that the erring crew-member was about to retire for a rest period wasn't sufficient reason for a stubbly chin and they would be sent off to shave at once. The real aggravation was having to report back so that he could check that they had done it properly.

But the current state of his face didn't bother Grant. Having shaved just before coming on duty, he knew he was safe even if the Captain did venture onto the bridge. But that was highly unlikely as they were in the middle of a crisis and the Captain, like all obsessive paranoid personalities, didn't like trouble which wasn't of his own making. Or at least didn't like to become involved. He preferred to shout and rant when the problem wasn't immediately solved. Such behaviour is common amongst people who have been promoted beyond their capabilities.

But none of this was in Grant's mind as he was more worried about the missing Chief Engineer. To be honest, he was more concerned about the search parties looking for the Chief Engineer. The computer had just annoyingly discovered an 'intruder' very close to his hoard of art treasures. At that very moment two members of the crew were trudging their reluctant way towards the sighting. All it required was for them to take a wrong turning and he would be in serious trouble.

The left side of Grant's nose began to itch. It always did when he was nervous – it was something else he didn't like about his acquired body. In fact, when it came to lying or practising any form of deception, he would start to twitch and itch and bob about like someone with St Vitus Dance.

Grant sat back in the big comfortable officer-of-the-watch chair and tried to relax. Worrying about things which had yet to occur had never been his style. Yet never before had he had so much to lose, and it was beginning to affect him. Not only did his nose still itch, but his stomach had begun to ache in sympathy. Silently Grant cursed whatever was in the ducting and the nervous disorder it was causing him.

Cardiac arrest was almost another condition to add to his list as the sudden sound of the intercom buzzer cut into his thoughts. Grant looked at the console and saw a tiny neon light above the talkback switch flash, demanding attention. It was one of the search parties in the ducting. The buzzer sounded again, its rasp twice as aggravating as usual.

Apprehensively Grant leant forward and pressed the switch. He was about to find out whether his treasure had been discovered. 'Bridge.'

'This is Bates.' The crewman's voice was calm, almost bored. 'If there's anything down here,' he continued, 'we can't find it.'

'Then try another area.' As Grant spoke he punched up on the VDU before him a plan of the sector Bates and his companion were searching. After studying it for a moment, he gave co-ordinates which would take them away from his hoard.

'But the computer said the intruder was in this area.' Bates's tone was now stubborn. He was tired of searching

34

and wanted to get out of the ducting. 'Can't we come up now? There's no-one down here.'

'Stay where you are!' Although Grant was desperate for the search party to clear the area, he had to be careful. For security reasons all conversations on the bridge were recorded. It was therefore vital for him not to appear too eager to call off the search. But then the answer occurred to him. The computer initiated the search, so he would let her sort it out. Grant smiled, his pains and twitches suddenly gone. He was being too careful. If his cache of treasures was found, it was likely that the Chief Engineer would be blamed. After all, the ducting was his area. Even if his swag were confiscated, he still had two years to 'reliberate' it.

Grant cleared his throat and said, 'Did you hear what Mr Bates said, computer? He can't find your intruder.'

The computer gave a small electronic bleep, then rattled into life. 'I did indeed. And it distresses me that poor Mr Bates and his companion are suffering on my account . . . '

Grant settled back in his chair. In recent months the computer had developed a verbosity which was verging on the unbearable. Instead of short, succinct reports, she would now waffle on for what seemed like hours, using twenty words when one would do. The computer had also taken to apologising a great deal and making excuses. It was becoming too human, almost neurotic.

Neither did the sound of her voice help much. In a moment of benevolence the Captain had insisted that it be reprogrammed. He said that he had had complaints from the crew who found it too strident and bossy. Grant had spent days trying to find a more agreeable sound, but whatever he came up with, the Captain didn't like. The voice was either too harsh or too soft; not authoritative enough; too sexy or not sexy enough. Always negative comments. Never any guide as to how it *should* sound.

Grant was almost at his wit's end, when the First Officer

happened to mention that the Captain was rather partial to Algolian women.

Now, the Algolian accent is not unlike New York American on Earth. This Grant could easily simulate. Needless to say the Captain liked it, but felt the voice needed a little more character. So Grant made it more chatty. The Captain loved it, but felt it required a little more refinement. This he undertook himself, working on the syntax and accent until it was exactly how he wanted. It now sounded like a demented, stereotyped, dizzy dame.

Unfortunately the rest of the crew hated it. But by then the Captain had forgotten that he had ordered it changed because of their complaint. Such is the power of command.

Grant let out a long yawn as the computer continued to chatter away. It was still apologising to Mr Bates.

'You've made your point,' snapped Grant. 'Mr Bates forgives you.'

'I'm so pleased to hear it.'

'Now, make his day and give him the precise location of the intruder. He's dying to meet him.'

The computer became silent. Grant feared she was building to another long discourse. 'Well,' she chirped at last, 'you must understand that I do not have visual contact with the intruder. I'm simply picking up a faint heat image through my infra-red fire warning sensors.'

'So what are they telling you now?'

'I'd rather not say.' She had started to sulk. 'It seems foolish to pass on inaccurate information. Bad data only lead to bad decisions . . .'

'Where is the intruder?' said Grant emphatically.

'Oh, very well, if you insist.' Again she paused, this time to check her sensor. 'Well,' she continued at last, 'as far as I can tell he is about ten metres away from Mr Bates.'

'Did you hear that?'

'Oh, yeah.' Bates sounded just as bored as before. 'That's a great deal of help.'

'I'm doing my best!' said the computer petulantly.

'Then I suggest you try a little harder. It's like a maze down here. You'll need to be a bit more precise.'

Again the computer became silent. She didn't like Bates's tone, but decided not to say anything. 'You could try behind the Bastik acid tanks.' But then added cautiously, 'As long as you accept that's only a suggestion. I will not be held responsible for what you might find.'

'What's that supposed to mean?' enquired Grant.

'You'll see.' The tone contained an edge of menace Grant had never heard the computer use before.

Down in the dark, gloomy ducting Bates and his companion, Wilson, had drawn their side arms and were cautiously making their way towards the Bastik acid tanks.

As they approached, they heard a soft growl. Bates turned his torch in the direction of the noise, but all they could see were the dense shadows created by the beam as it passed over the acid containers.

Silently, Bates indicated to Wilson that he should take left side of the tanks while he made his way around to the right. Hopefully they would trap the creature in a pincer movement and kill it with their cross fire. They had no intention of trying to take it alive.

But it wasn't to be.

Bates shone his torch into the shadows. The darkness under the tanks seemed to be thicker, denser, blacker. He knew it was all in his imagination but that didn't reassure him. Carefully he lined up his gun and torch, one above the other. Then slowly he started to pan the beam of light across the area before him. If anything was caught in it, all he then needed to do was to squeeze the gun's trigger and it would be dead.

At least that was the classroom theory. But out in the hard, dark, cold world of the ducting he wasn't so certain it would be that easy. Especially as this was the first time he had ever had to kill anything.

Slowly Bates edged forward, continuing to sweep the area ahead with his torch. *So far so good.* But hadn't the man who had fallen from an eighty storey building said the same thing as he passed each floor? Perhaps the character in that apocryphal tale wouldn't have been quite so confident if he had been familiar with another old aphorism – it isn't the fall that hurts but coming to a sudden stop at the bottom.

Bates continued to advance. He was now more than half way around the tanks and becoming concerned as to the whereabouts of Wilson.

Suddenly there was a noise, like a boot scuffing against a steel plate. Bates turned in the direction of the sound, but could see nothing but deep unfriendly shadows.

As Bates turned away he heard the sound again, only this time a little closer.

Desperate for reassurance that his colleague was safe, Bates risked calling to him. No reply. He called again, and this time was answered by another scuff.

Bates rushed towards a particularly dense entanglement of tank legs from where the sound seemed to emanate. As he approached, the beam of his torch was deflected from the entanglement, creating shadows which pranced and jigged like manic spectres over the nearby wall of the ducting. If Bates had been a little less scared, a little more in control of himself, he would have noticed that one of the shadows wasn't moving quite like the others.

On reaching the struts, Bates paused to listen again. Silence. Once more he called Wilson's name. Still no reply. He then started to fumble for the radio clipped to his waist. *I must get help!* As he unsnapped the transceiver from its mount, he heard another sound, this time to his right.

Bates swung round and the beam of his torch settled on a familiar face. It was Wilson. Bates momentarily relaxed, pleased that his colleague was safe. It was a full second before he realised that all he was staring at was a head perched on a

38

metal spar. The rest of Wilson was missing, ripped off at the neck.

Unable to control himself any longer, Bates let out a terrible scream, turned and started to run. But he didn't get very far.

As he rushed past the steelwork of the tanks, a powerful arm reached out and grabbed him by the neck. Locked in a powerful grip, he was lifted clear of the floor and dangled, helplessly, like a hanged man.

The last thing Bates ever heard was his own neck breaking. He never felt the impact as he was thrown to the floor. Neither did his dead eyes see his murderer as he emerged from the metalwork. He was past caring. And in a few minutes all that would remain of him would be his boots. If Bates had been aware of this gruesome fact, he wouldn't have taken the trouble to have washed that morning.

Up on the bridge Grant sat filing his offending nail. He had yet to learn what had happened. When the computer finally did inform him, his only concern was for his hidden treasure.

But something occurred to distract him from his immediate worries. The Captain had sent for him.

And according to the computer, he was in a very bad mood.

4

'This is the Captain of Your Ship . . . '

As we now know, eighty-seven per cent of all life in the universe is carbon-based. Of that percentage, more than half is humanoid in form.

The crew of the *Vipod Mor* were all humanoid and the majority carbon-based. But there was also a group, an elite minority, as they saw themselves, who were quartz-based.

Physiologically there wasn't an awful lot of difference between the two species, both having lungs, kidneys, livers, and the like, or at least organs which performed similar functions. The inhalation of gases necessary for a healthy life was the same, except that 'quartz' required more helium, creating for their 'carbon' colleagues the side effect of a quarter octave rise in the normal timbre of the voice.

In appearance, 'quartz' was more like a re-edited version of 'carbon' rather than different. Their craniums were much larger than 'carbons' with an extended, dome-like frontal lobe. This had the effect of pushing their eyes down onto their cheeks, which in turn placed their mouth where 'carbons' chin would be.

It was fortunate quartz-based life forms didn't go in for chins much, except when grossly overweight, as their necks continued down to their shoulders at much the same circumference as the lower half of their heads. This gave the effect of an oblong face balanced on a broad shelf of shoulders.

All quartz-based life forms have tiny, purple, almond-shaped eyes, with equally minute mouths which contain three rows of sharp, needle-like teeth. This is very odd as they are physiologically committed to be vegetarians – their bodies are unable to digest meat. By rights, their teeth should be of the flat, chewing kind and not the carnivorous razors they had evolved. As their teeth are unsuitable for their diet they often develop digestive problems later in life.

On the whole 'quartz' is shorter and stockier than their 'carbon' cousin, yet tend to weigh the same. As this extra body bulk is entirely muscle, they tend to be much stronger than other life forms.

Unlike the layered epidermis of 'carbon', their skin grows in large, thick nodules the size of small turnips. Whatever the colour of their skin – be it mauve, purple, blue or, of course, green – it was always completely hairless and as hard and as glazed as a ceramic tile.

Captain Orlous Moston Slarn, master of the *Vipod Mor*, was a quartz-based life form. Even if he had known this he wouldn't have been interested. In fact, Slarn wasn't interested in anything except pleasure. His own self-indulgent pleasure, that was, and no-one else's. As far as he was concerned the universe existed to satisfy *him*. If he didn't go to bed each night having experienced ten original pleasures, he wanted to know why.

It must be understood that being totally selfish was not a characteristic of quartz-based people – just Slarn. In fact, he was more than selfish, he was repulsive both in appearance and manner.

No-one aboard the *Vipod Mor* understood why he had been appointed captain. He wasn't an engineer or a guidance expert as most Captains were. In fact, he knew nothing about how the ship functioned. But worse still, he didn't care about his ignorance.

Slarn had started his professional career as an entertainments officer aboard the Starliner, the *SS Vampon*. Why anyone had employed him was yet another great mystery.

Again, it wasn't that he knew anything about how to organise shipboard entertainments, nor that he was particularly amusing or entertaining in himself. The reason he had inflicted himself on this branch of the service was simply because he enjoyed going to parties.

Of course, being an officer, he expected others to organise the events, do the catering, arrange the music. He felt his function was simply to shout a lot and be thoroughly unpleasant if the event did not come up to his exacting standards. Whether the passengers enjoyed themselves was unimportant. The event was only considered a success if *he* had.

It must be said, though, that Slarn was very good at two things: writing memos; and dodging the flying globules of fat *after* they had hit the fan.

For example, if passengers complained about the tediousness of a party, or the general standard of the entertainment, he was the first to agree. Inevitably he would put his outrage into a well-worded memo to the purser – with a copy to the captain – denouncing the incompetence of some minion.

During his first cruise, and on his say-so alone, the whole entertainments staff was sacked and replaced four times. No one in authority seemed to notice that the real problem was Slarn. Of course, this couldn't last. When, on further voyages, someone in authority did notice his incompetences, Slarn was always careful to resign and move on. If the captain didn't give him a good reference, then he would write his own.

How he was nominated for his captaincy is interesting only in as much as it is a good example of how being in the right place at the right time, then bending events to your advantage, can bring about the elevation of an incompetent.

The incident occurred one fateful night about two years after Slarn had bribed his way to the rank of purser. Like the *Titanic* of long ago Earth history, a new, super-luxurious, ultra-safe starliner was on its maiden voyage.

Suddenly the sensors picked up a swarm of meteors dead ahead. Confident his force shield could resist even the impact of a small planet, the Captain ordered they continue at full speed.

Needless to say, the craft was split in two. Although the main part of the ship was destroyed, the gas-tight safety doors held on the ballroom section, granting the panic-stricken survivors a few extra hours of life.

However, the crew's spirit sank when it was discovered that the only officer still alive was Slarn. If anyone was to survive this tragedy, it was vital that order be restored. Slarn wasn't interested. If he was about to die, he didn't want to waste his time looking after others.

Fortunately, a young stewardess, endowed with a presence of mind and quality of leadership which sent Slarn into a paroxysm of paranoia, escorted one of the less terrified male passengers to the dance floor. Seeing what the steward-ess had in mind, the band leader brought what was left of his orchestra to order and they started to play.

Such was the passengers' surprise on hearing the music, they quietened down. As they did, they noticed the young stewardess and her partner dancing, and such was the couple's serenity and confidence, it inspired others to join them and soon the dance floor was packed.

Calm and order had been restored!

When the passengers were finally rescued, they had nothing but praise for the crew, but, alas, their relief at still being alive had erased the memory of Slarn's insidious cowardice.

Although it was too risky for him to claim the direct credit, Slarn realised that, if he were to bathe in any of the reflected glory, he would also have to praise the crew's efforts, yet subtly imply they were acting under his direct and inspired leadership.

Of course, he succeeded. When the official enquiry into

the accident delivered its report, the young stewardess, or her part in the events, wasn't even mentioned. It was Orlous Slarn who was the hero!

After that, he went from strength to strength. A year later he was offered the captaincy of the first ship he had served on, the *SS Vampon*.

Now, it must be understood that captains of starliners, unlike battle cruisers or deep space freighters, do not require a rigorous training in the ship's functions. At least in Setna they don't. As their cargo is rich passengers who demand to be coddled and pampered, it is more important for the captain to be skilled in the art of public relations.

Although Slarn even lacked good manners, he was, at first, sensible enough to surround himself with young officers who would work hard, yet not cast any shadows upon him. He also thought that their youth would make them more pliable when it came to having to cope with his megalo-maniacal, self-indulgent behaviour.

At least that is what he hoped.

But, of course, such corruption couldn't last unnoticed for ever. Even as a child, Slarn had had to learn this lesson.

When younger, Orlous Moston Slarn had been a brat of unprecedented arrogance. Whatever the cost he always had to have his way. Although his parents were manically indulgent, it was never to a sufficiently humiliating standard that satisfied him. He would therefore spend hours working on new ways to provoke them into even more degrading compromises.

Then one day, purely by chance, he discovered the most effective form of manipulation: illness. The sicker he became, the more they gave in to him. Of course, being *really* ill was unpleasant and dangerous. Pretending to be unwell was equally dangerous because of the chance of discovery.

It was then that Orlous discovered he could simulate all the symptoms of a disease by simple will power. This, of course, eliminated all the unpleasantness, risks and side

44

effects. After all, he didn't want to compromise himself by doing something silly like *really* dying.

At first he experimented with milder complaints, perfecting each and every medical detail. He then expanded his repertoire to include 'safe' frighteners such as Spandau Sickness and a particularly unpleasant bowel complaint known as the Boils of Heydron.

Such was the accuracy of his symptoms that one day, while perfecting the Curse of Hogus, he infected his brother, who promptly died.

Slarn was delighted. He now possessed the ultimate weapon. Anyone who aggravated or wouldn't let him have his own way was promptly infected with the most unpleasant and deadly condition he could simulate.

By the time he was fifteen years old he was an orphan, having 'murdered' his whole family. Yet he himself had hardly had a genuine day's illness in his life, seeming to be immune to his own menace.

But as Slarn grew older, he found he was unable to use his unique skill as freely as he wished. When you're young and unwell, you are an object of sympathy. As an adult, you soon become a bit of a pest and people are quick to lock you up in an isolation hospital, or worse still, a lunatic asylum.

Of course Slarn didn't want that, although he belonged in one or the other, so he decided to give up being 'ill' and become a verbal bully instead.

That was until he became a captain of a starliner.

Now, it must be understood that such people are very much a law unto themselves. They are solely in charge of their ships and the arbiter of all things. Because one person holds so much power, such people are usually selected very carefully, after having gained much experience about the craft they are to command and having proved their capabilities as *stable* leaders. Slarn, of course, had evaded both this intense form of training and vetting.

Once he realised he couldn't control his keen, young

45

officers any longer he had had them replaced with older types, who were afraid of being dismissed. This meant that Slarn could develop his campaign of abuse – something he now seemed to need like an addictive drug – in the safe knowledge that there would be very little resistance.

It was at this time that Orlous Moston Slarn returned to the methods he had used as a child.

On the whole, the crew behaved themselves very well, working hard and executing their duty with due care and attention to detail. But this wasn't enough for Slarn. He expected adoration along with everything else. And if he didn't get it, he would become very 'ill' indeed.

Of course, Slarn was always fair – at least from his point of view – in the diseases he selected as punishment. A small misdemeanour meant a few days in the sick bay with 'Weedle's Fever'. A more gross act of indiscipline would be met with a bout of 'Vex's Syndrome', which often necessitated a complete lung transplant if the patient were to make a total recovery. Any crewmember who was foolish enough to become recalcitrant would receive a visitation from Narn's Pox or Moriarty's Revenge, two highly contagious infections which demanded immediate transfer to an isolation hospital, where slowly and very painfully they would die.

But even if the crew seemed to be behaving themselves, Slarn would unleash a bout of 'something' just to keep them on their toes. How he managed to get away with his despicable behaviour was a total mystery – but he did. When he retired, it was with full pension and a 'Hero of Command' medal, first class.

When the committe who were organising the voyage of the *Vipod Mor* came to chose a captain, they had decided they wanted someone experienced in public relations, someone used to handling quirky, demanding people. After all, the bulk of the crew would be made up of scientists, geologists, anthropologists, archaeologists – specialists of all kinds. It wouldn't do, they reasoned, to have a seasoned freighter captain, used to sailing his ship by the seat of his pants, experienced only in handling a rough, tough crew. They wanted someone with tact, decorum and understanding, someone used to organising demanding, discerning members of the public.

Somehow Slarn's name came up. His experience aboard a starliner made him a perfect candidate and he was added to the shortlist.

Three days before all the nominees were to be interviewed, they contracted Bexel's Syndome and died. That was, of course, with the exception of Slarn. No-one on the committee found this at all curious or suspicious, even though Bexel's Syndome was supposed to have been eradicated from the galaxy.

As Slarn was the only surviving member of those short-listed, he was appointed captain. He was happy again, as once more he had a ship to terrorise.

PART TWO

. . . Goodnight and Amen

5

The Dissolute Time Lord

Aboard the TARDIS, things were very quiet. In the case of the Doctor, they were very peaceful indeed. In fact, they were positively soporific: he was sound asleep.

As a rule, Time Lords require far less sleep than most humanoid life forms, usually managing to survive quite happily on three hours a day. What's more, they also have the advantage of not requiring to take their rest in bulk. A ten minute doze here, a half hour snooze there, is a valid contribution to their three hour quota.

Under normal circumstances, the Doctor would sleep in a like manner, but on this particular occasion, he had been dead to everything for over eight hours. The reason for this was quite simple: he was drunk.

Now, it must be stressed that the Doctor is very moderate when it comes to alcohol, partaking of the occasional glass only at Christmas, on his birthday or some other special occasion. In many respects this makes him rather naive when it comes to alcohol, and when someone, as had occurred on this occasion, continued to refill his glass he was unaware of the likely consequences. This may be difficult to believe in a nine hundred year old Time Lord, but then there are many strange aberrations in the Doctor's experience, the explanation of which is best left to his 'official' biography.

The current intoxicated state of the Doctor's had come about on Zaurak Minor in the self-same Voxnic bar where Grant had met Oliver Sneed. How the Doctor and his

American companion Peri had finished up there was brought about by a common occurrence in their lives: they were lost. Once more the TARDIS's navigation system had failed, necessitating the materialisation on the nearest, inhabited planet.

As Peri had never been to a Voxnic bar before, and as Zaurak boasts of some of the finest in its corner of the universe, the Doctor decided it was time to broaden her education.

After careful consideration, they found themselves in a small, dimly lit bar which catered mainly for the crews of passing space freighters. It was called Lucan's Place, named after a famous fugitive from Earth.

As the duo lowered themselves onto thin, spindly stools at the bar, a chatty, three-headed Vospodian placed beakers of Voxnic before them. While the Doctor exchanged pleasantries with their hostess, Peri gazed around.

The room was packed with all kinds of different life forms. In one corner was a group of Ninson Warriors, considered by some to be the most sadistic and ferocious soldiers in the universe. Yet on this occasion, they sat quietly, chatting amongst themselves and quaffing tankards of their favourite brew. Nearby, and equally content with life, were half a dozen Terileptils tucking into a snack of Viston seeds and scarnel nibblets.

In another part of the room were a group of Droogniks. They were the strangest sight of all, with their purple-crested, constantly nodding heads. Drinking was always a problem for them, for not only did their heads nod, but their hands oscillated, which made contact between beaker and mouth a very tricky problem indeed.

Peri smiled. She felt happy. The atmosphere was relaxed and friendly. Everyone seemed to be having a good time and she wished that all the places they visited could be so pleasant.

As Peri sipped her Voxnic, she watched the Vospodian

52

waitresses as they slipped nimbly between the tables, refilling the customers' empty beakers.

It was then that she noticed three humanoid life forms seated in a far corner of the room. One of them was very drunk and, although she couldn't hear what was being said, his two companions seemed to be shouting at him.

Peri withdrew her gaze. She wasn't in the mood to have the atmosphere spoilt by people bickering; she was enjoying herself too much for that.

On the other hand, she might have paid more attention if she had known the man who was drunk went under the name of Oliver Sneed, the surgeon who had transplanted Shellingborne Grant's brain into another body. She would have paid even more attention if she had known that the two men haranguing him were officers of the Setna Interplanetary Police Force, for in the not too distant future, they would also give her a very hard time.

But there wasn't any way she could have known that, so Peri continued to sit contentedly on her spindly stool, sipping her drink.

While his companion had been enjoying the atmosphere of Lucan's Place, the Doctor had continued his conversation with the Vospodian hostess. Such had been the tantalising nature of their dialogue, he hadn't noticed how quickly he had consumed his Voxnic. More to the point, neither was he aware of how intently his beaker was being refilled.

The moment of truth didn't come until he made a sudden move. It was then that he learnt he was no longer in full control of his balance or the limbs of his body. One moment he had been perched agreeably on his stool; the next he was sprawling on the floor.

Once Peri had come to terms with the embarrassment of a nine hundred year old drunken Time Lord her main concern was how she was going to get him back to the TARDIS. The Doctor wasn't the smallest of men and she certainly couldn't lift or carry him.

Fortunately, one of the Terileptils came to her rescue. His name was Danstop and he was a life support maintenance engineer aboard a freighter which shipped tinclavic ore from the Terileptil mines on Raaga.

As Danstop effortlessly carried the Doctor back to the TARDIS, he told Peri about how boring his job was and how he only did it because it paid so well; about how he missed his wife and children and that if he had had his way he would have preferred to have been a poet or a circus clown. (Both these professions were venerated by the Terileptils). But as he didn't have any talent for either activity, he had to content himself with being a life support maintenance engineer.

Danstop reminded Peri of the sort of person she occasionally met on Earth in the subway. They too would waffle on about their lives in an uninhibited way, showing little concern for the inflicted listener.

But as it turned out, he was friendly enough, simply a lonely person who wanted someone to talk to and for a moment share the burden of his loneliness.

With the Doctor tucked up in bed, Danstop returned to his companions at the Voxnic bar. But he had no sooner gone than the Doctor sat bolt upright; muttering some instructions at Peri, then collapsed back onto his pillow.

Peri wandered back into the TARDIS console room and stared at the instruments before her. She suddenly felt sad and lonely. Her evening had been ruined, the good feelings she had felt earlier now a distant memory. *Why does he always manage to spoil my fun?* As the Doctor never did this on purpose, there probably wasn't a very satisfactory answer.

Peri forced her sadness to the back of her mind and instead wondered whether she should implement the Doctor's instructions or wait for him to sober up.

Although she knew little about the complex procedures for flying the TARDIS, her understanding was enough to know that she had been asked to programme co-ordinates – for where she did not know – and then set the time rotor in action.

Alternatively, Peri thought, naughtily, she could leave the Doctor to sleep it off and go back to Lucan's Place. But she didn't. Instead, reluctantly, she set the time-machine in motion, knowing that if she left the Doctor unattended, he might get into even more trouble. At least in the depths of space he would be safe and out of harm's way.

As things turned out, Peri couldn't have been more mistaken. But then, as always, how could she have known otherwise?

The Doctor tossed and turned. Until a few minutes ago, he had been resting peacefully. Now something was disturbing him and he felt as though he were awake, yet knew he was in a dream.

As he wriggled and twisted, reducing his blankets to the appearance of a compressed concertina, his mind was filled with shrill, harsh sounds. It was as though a Ninhana symphony orchestra was deliberately detuning its instruments. As anyone familiar with Ninhana music will know, even when played perfectly, it is the most excruciating sound imaginable. It has since been outlawed on most planets, and is only ever allowed as a grotesque form of capital punishment for particularly sadistic villains.

The few Earth people who have had the misfortune of attending a Ninhana concert have likened the incident to an incompetent dentist attacking an infected cavity with a rusty nail while having the soles of your feet tickled. Only far worse. It is said that the likes of Samson would have shaved his own head rather than experience such sounds. And that Lot's wife would not only have willingly been turned into a pillar of salt, but also provided the potato crisps to go with it.

This was what the Doctor was experiencing. Or had been. For the sound had stopped as suddenly as it had started and

55

in its place could be heard the distinctive quality of a woman's voice.

At first it was too distant to understand what she was saying. Even as it grew louder, it still ebbed and flowed like the transmission of an under-powered radio. Yet in spite of the interference, there was an undeniable urgency about the voice which demanded attention.

'Summoning up all his effort, the Doctor called: 'I can't hear you. You must speak more clearly.'

There was a long pause, then the voice said much louder: 'Time . . . Time . . . The eclipse of time . . . '

What's she talking about? was the Doctor's immediate response, but he checked himself, aware that everything he thought might be conveyed to the owner of the voice. And the last thing he wanted to do was frighten her away, especially after the pain he had suffered. 'You're not making sense,' he said urgently. 'I don't know what you mean. Please be more precise.'

'Time . . . ' the voice intoned. 'Full circle . . . Things must be allowed to turn full circle.'

As the Doctor tried to make sense of the message, he became aware of another female voice. This too had an urgency about it along with a familiarity he couldn't quite place. The Doctor wondered what was happening to him. *Two* women in the *same* dream, *both* with urgent messages. Things were looking up.

The Time Lord struggled to eliminate the flippancy from his thoughts. As he could only cope with one voice at a time, he decided the second one could wait. 'Try once more,' he said to the original voice. 'Please tell me what you want.'

But before it could answer, his body started to jerk from side to side, as though being tugged at by a pack of scavenging dogs.

The Doctor struggled desperately to hang onto his dream, but contact was being inhibited by the constant penetrating call of 'Doctor! Doctor!'

56

Then as suddenly as the original voice had arrived, it was gone. It took a full ten seconds for the Doctor to realise why: he was awake.

And very hungover.

Slowly he opened his bloodshot eyes and allowed acid-tipped shafts of light to attack the retinas. As the pain eased, the muscles which controlled his focus slowly, searingly started to function and a familiar face came into view: it was Peri's.

With all the care a nurse brings to moving a fracture case, the Doctor manoeuvred his body into a sitting position. He had only once before felt this dreadful. That had been after a moment of foolish bravado when he had queried the loss of his no-claims bonus on the TARDIS with a Setchnik claims assessor.

Carefully the Doctor opened his lips and tried to speak, but the piece of concrete in his mouth failed to function. Convinced his tongue had atrophied, he started to panic. Fear can often be a great reviver and this occasion was no exception. Very slowly life returned to his oral member and his mouth began to generate saliva.

'What do you think you're doing?' The Doctor wanted to sound angry, but his voice came out as though his mouth was full of paper tissue.

Peri stared down at the wreck before her: 'What do you think I was doing? Waking you up!'

Somehow her reply seemed too logical for the Doctor's addled brain to assess. 'I wish you hadn't,' he bleated. 'I had a voice inside my head.'

'Well, I'm sorry to interrupt your dreaming,' said Peri. 'It's just that something rather frightening has happened.'

The Doctor didn't reply. His mind was still full of the echoes of the voice he had heard. He knew the memory of it was too real to have been a dream. It was as though someone was trying to project their thoughts into his mind. It was important for Peri to understand that. But then, he recalled what had happened in the Voxnic bar and knew that after his behaviour she would never believe him ever again.

'Well?' Peri's shrill voice cut into his thoughts. 'Don't you want to know what's happened?'

Racked with guilt, the Doctor nodded.

'The TARDIS has materialised,' she said. 'We're still in deep space! Alongside an enormous spaceship!'

The Time Lord raised an eyebrow, found it too heavy, and lowered it again. *Already?* Yet the clock on the wall told him he hadn't been asleep long enough for them to have reached their destination.

With all the control he could manage, the Doctor swung his legs slowly over the side of the bed and rested his feet on the floor. He knew it was going to be a very hard day.

'I wouldn't have bothered you,' continued Peri, 'if the console hadn't started doing all sorts of strange things.'

'Such as?'

'Everything! It went mad! It started to wink, flash and grunt like some dirty old man in a park!'

The Doctor raised his other eyebrow at the rather graphic description, and instantly knew that if he wasn't going to wear himself out, he would have to refrain from all this facial activity.

'That's why I woke you up,' Peri insisted. 'I was scared!'

'Interesting,' the Doctor mused.

'That I was scared?'

'That I should hear a voice as the TARDIS makes an impromptu materialisation.'

As Peri helped the Doctor along the corridor towards the console room, she was at a loss to understand how a voice induced by alcohol poisoning could have anything to do with what had occurred.

As the duo entered the console room, the Doctor risked abandoning Peri's support. Carefully, and very slowly, he shuffled around the console examining dials, flicking switches and pressing buttons.

At long last he said, 'Everything seems to be in order.'

'It wasn't a few minutes ago,' Peri reminded him.

The Doctor believed her, but omitted to say so, which left Peri feeling a little silly, given all the fuss she had made.

Yet on this occasion the Doctor could be forgiven for being inconsiderate as he was somewhat preoccupied about the state of the TARDIS. Materialising before reaching its preprogrammed destination was not only a new fault, but a particularly dangerous one. Although the shell of the time-machine was designed to resist run of the mill aggravations such as laser fire and meteor collision, it wasn't totally impervious. If the ship were to materialise at the heart of a star – something its preprogramming was supposed to prevent – it would instantly vaporise. But as the TARDIS seemed to have decided to materialise at whim, its destruction had become an uncomfortable possibility.

The Doctor scratched his head. 'This noise you heard – what did it sound like?'

Peri thought for a moment. As it was unlike any other she had experienced, it was difficult to describe. So she said so.

'Try and show me,' prompted the Doctor.

Peri inhaled, and as she forced the compressed air through her larynx, the sound which emanated was similar to that of an actively flatulent herbivore with undertones of a distressed musk.

The Doctor was impressed with her vocal dexterity, but was still none the wiser. 'Are you sure it was like that?' he asked.

Peri exploded. 'You don't think I could invent such a stupid noise?'

As she spoke, the sound was heard again, this time from the console. 'That's it!' she cried.

The Doctor looked very grave. In fact, such was his concern it caused his hangover to clear. 'This is very bad news,' he said. 'It's what caused the TARDIS to materialise. The claxon indicated time spillage.' The Doctor looked at the image of the freighter on the scanner screen. 'Someone on board that ship must be illegally experimenting with time.'

Peri understood little about the Laws of Time, but knew that when they were interfered with all sorts of unpleasant effects occurred concerning the established history of the past and future. It wasn't without reason that the Time Lords of Gallifrey had outlawed such experiments.

The Doctor knew this and, as much as the thought disturbed him, he would have to board the freighter, find and stop whoever was conducting the experiments.

He suddenly felt very ill again. It was going to be a very hard day indeed, the sort that would require more than two aspirin . . .

6

Bath Time

It was not without some trepidation that Shellingborne Grant approached the door of the Captain's cabin. Even with a past as dark and as murky as his, he was still a little afraid of Slarn.

Yet during this voyage, the Captain had not always had his own way. Few of the specialised crew were afraid of his blustering, bullying ways. Some of them were too eccentric even to notice that he performed as he did. Neither could Slarn freely infect anyone he took umbrage against, as many of the scientists were irreplaceable. This meant that his paranoid outbursts had to be restricted to his junior officers and maintenance members of the crew.

Grant was such a crewmember, and, although until now he had managed to avoid the Captain's wrath, he felt that he could have run out of luck.

Cautiously Grant knocked on the door. Silently it slid open and he was ushered into an outer office by Velsper, Slarn's steward.

Like the captain, Velsper was a quartz-based life form. Also like the Captain, he was grossly overweight, and rather unpleasant to carbon-based life forms. The reason for his behaviour, unlike that of the Captain, was simple – he was a racist.

Grant knew this, but didn't care. What did bother him was the influence he had with the Captain, as it was

rumoured he had 'fingered' half the crew who had subse-
quently become very 'ill'. Velsper wasn't someone you
aggravated, not unless you had the telephone numbers of
several good doctors.

'And how are we today?' smarmed Velsper, in his usual
excessive manner.

'I'm fine,' said Grant concerned at the sudden interest in
his health.

'You certainly look very well . . . Which is more than can
be said for the poor Captain.'

This wasn't a good beginning. 'How *unwell* is he?' asked
Grant.

The steward removed a surgical gown from its sterilised
wrapping and offered it to Grant. '*Very* unwell, sir. You
know how personally the Captain takes everything.'

As Grant struggled into the gown, he noticed that he had
started to perspire.

'In fact, he's so poorly,' continued Velsper, 'I've had to
confine him to a lava bath.'

That unwell! screamed Grant in the depths of his mind.

The steward unpacked a surgical mask and handed it to
Grant. 'I can tell you, sir,' he said, 'it hasn't been a very
pleasant morning . . . What's more, I fear this afternoon
could be far worse.'

In spite of feeling hot, a cold shiver travelled down the
length of Grant's body. 'Has he developed any symptoms?'

'It's very difficult to say, sir. You know how unpredict-
able stress-related diseases can be. I mean, they can manifest
themselves in the most surprising way.'

Grant knew that only too well. The last time the Captain
had been 'ill' he had developed a plague of boils and, by
mistake, passed the infection on to the entire sick bay staff.

'One can only hope,' said Velsper, 'that whatever he is
incubating doesn't spread to the rest of the crew. Even when
isolated, contagious infection is very difficult to contain.'

'So I've noticed.' Grant's voice was now muffled behind

the surgical mask. 'The crew no sooner go down with the complaint he has psychosomatically created, than he gets better.'

'I know, sir,' said Velsper as he made his way across the room to a large, hermetically sealed door. 'The Captain has an amazing constitution, sir.'

'*Conveniently* so.'

Grant hadn't meant his comment to sound quite so critical and his tone did not go unnoticed by Velsper. He curled his top lip and thrust forward his bottom set of needle-sharp teeth in the way quartz-based people do when annoyed. 'Then let's hope you have sufficiently good news to prevent further deterioration,' he snapped.

As the hermetically sealed door slid open, billows of hot, sulphurous gas tumbled from the room beyond, like so many students from a telephone box during rag week.

Velsper indicated that Grant should enter the smog, and on so doing, the door crashed shut behind him.

Grant felt decidedly uneasy. Somewhere to his left, he could hear the bubbling, hot lava. Never having been in the Captain's bathroom before, he was uncertain of the geography and wasn't keen to risk a recce, given that the thick clouds of dense sulphur made it impossible to see more than a few centimetres in any direction. One false move and he could join the Captain in his bath. If the sight of his naked leader didn't induce a cardiac arrest, then the boiling lava certainly would.

Grant started to cough as the sulphur irritated his lungs.

'Is that you, Mr Grant?' The voice was deep, resonant. It also belonged to the Captain.

'Yes, sir.'

'Where are you?'

'By the door, sir.'

'Advance, so that I can see you.'

Grant edged forward a little, then lost his nerve. 'I can't see where I'm going, sir.'

'Step into the light, Mister!' snapped Slarn. 'I am your Captain and I wish to *see* as well as *hear* you fawn!'

Grant took a few more tentative steps, but the visibility didn't improve. 'I'd like to comply with your order, sir, but everytime I move, the smoke seems to follow.'

Slarn let out a deep, threatening roar. 'Understand this, Mister, I do not encourage the development of charismatic personalities amongst my junior officers.'

'Absolutely, sir.'

'So vacate that cloud at once! Or take the consequences of your insubordination.'

There was just enough genuine menace in Slarn's voice to galvanise Grant into action. Without thinking of the possible consequences, he advanced, his eyes tightly closed. As it turned out, this was a foolish thing to do, as he became completely disorientated. Instead of manoeuvring towards his hateful leader, he started to travel away.

Down in the ducting, things were a little less silly, although, as it would turn out, just as dangerous.

The TARDIS had arrived and Peri and the Doctor were cautiously looking around. 'It's spooky,' said Peri. 'Why do you always find the most inhospitable places to park?'

The Doctor stared through the gloom at his companion. *Why does she always ask the same cretinous question everytime we arrive somewhere new?* 'Usual reason,' he said, sauntering off along the ducting. 'I want to have a look around before I announce my presence.'

The Doctor heard the clack of heel against metal as Peri ran to catch him up. 'What will you do when you find the people responsible for the time experiments?' she asked.

'Inform them of the danger. Advise them of the fact that such experiments are highly illegal.'

'And if they don't listen?'

Again, another familiar question. *I shall put out their eyes with hot pokers and cut their hands off! What do you think I'll do?*

'The usual thing . . . improvise.'

The duo strolled on, the sounds of the ship echoing like some electronic Trivolian symphony along the ducting. Occasionally there would be a harsher sound, like a massive voltage of electricity leaping between two conducters. This jarred on the duo's nerves and was made especially painful as the noise came at irregular intervals, making it impossible to anticipate.

Yet this was a minor inconvenience when compared with the lighting, as each lamp had been set at such an angle that it generated a minimum amount of light. Neither did it help that the ducting had been coated in a matt black finish, as this seemed to drink what illumination there was, and at the same time create shadows within shadows.

It was these denser spectral centres which caused Peri and the Doctor most problems, as, when caught in the periphery of their vision, they conjured up grotesque, evil images.

But these were fantasies of the imagination, which, although inconvenient, were ultimately harmless. The roar which echoed down the ducting was quite the reverse: it was real and belonged to the creature which had already killed and eaten three of the *Vipod Mor*'s crew.

The Doctor and Peri turned towards the source of the sound. Running from shadow to shadow, with an ease and speed which would soon put the creature within their immediate proximity, was a large shape made more menacing by the fact that it could only be seen in silhouette. On its own planet, the creature was known as a Maston, a piece of information which interested neither of the duo at that precise moment. Their only concern was whether they could outrun him, as the creature's demeanour and general attitude more than suggested brutal – if not terminal – intentions.

The Doctor and Peri turned and fled, forced away from the TARDIS by the pursuing Maston. As they ran, the Doctor noticed there were smaller, narrower passages leading off the main ducting and wondered whether an escape route lay in any of them. To try and outrun a creature who was gaining on them by the second was foolish, as it was only a matter of time before one of them would be clubbed down. The Doctor knew this and was aware that he must immediately take some form of evasive action.

Like a manic hitchhiker, he jerked his thumb towards one of the side tunnels ahead, indicating to Peri that they should turn into it. This she did and they found themselves in a smaller, lower section of ducting.

As the much bulkier Maston followed, he found himself impeded by the restricted space, and was forced to reduce his speed. This in turn allowed Peri and the Doctor to settle into a gentle jog, a pace they could more happily sustain.

'Shouldn't you talk to it?' panted Peri. 'Convince it we don't mean it any harm.'

The creature roared, and its anger bounced and ricocheted off the walls of the metal tunnel.

'I get the feeling it has only one thought in its mind,' replied the Time Lord, 'and that is, which one of us to eat first!'

The time-travellers jogged on in silence. Once they had lost the Maston they would have to find a route back to the TARDIS. *How*, of course, was a different matter, as neither of them had any idea of the layout of the ship.

Although he should have known better, the Doctor didn't feel too down-hearted with their situation. 'You know,' he said, 'I once met a man at a party who had found himself in a position not dissimilar to our own. As I recall, his name was Rudolph Musk.'

Peri glanced at the Time Lord and wondered whether he had finally cracked under the strain. 'Is this really a suitable time for a story?' she asked.

'Can't think of anything else I would prefer to do,' he said airily.

Given the matter-of-factness of his statement, juxtaposed

to the bizarrreness of their situation, Peri couldn't think of a suitably profound answer. So instead she glanced over her shoulder at their pursuer. In spite of the encumbrance of the restrictive tunnel, he was still gaining on them. Peri hoped it would be a short story. She would hate to die not knowing how it ended.

The Doctor took a deep breath and told of how, while walking in a forest on Veegal Minor, Rudolph Musk had been swallowed whole by a splay-footed sceeg, a ferocious animal with a mouth the size of a horse box.

Given their present situation, Peri was uncertain whether this was the sort of story she wanted to hear. Foolishly she had hoped for something more uplifting, or, at least, something more comforting.

The Doctor continued to drone on. It seemed that as Rudolph was slowly sliding down the sceeg's gullet, he thought that he would spend his last remaining seconds reciting his favourite sonnet – *Ode to a Flashist Mud Scavenger!* Peri's heart sunk as the Doctor launched into a recitation of the Ode. Such was his breathy, lack-lustre rendering, that it almost brought tears to her eyes, which ironically was the similar effect it had had on the sceeg, only in his case, the mucus in his gullet had evaporated and he had been forced to regurgitate Rudolph or choke. Peri wasn't surprised as she was feeling a similar discomfort herself. Perhaps being eaten wouldn't be so bad after all, she thought. At least she would never have to listen to any more of the Doctor's bad stories.

'Why did you just tell me that?' she enquired rather gracelessly.

The Doctor looked down his now perspiring nose at his companion. 'It was in the apparent vain hope that it would reassure you,' he said stiffly.

'Only if our pursuer finds your story as indigestible as I did,' she retorted. 'Perhaps you should tell it to him.'

As she spoke, the length of ducting they were jogging along suddenly broadened and became higher. They had come to the end of their respite. Behind them, the Maston roared as though in celebration.

The duo increased their pace, but it was apparent that they wouldn't be able to sustain it for long. Peri looked back at the creature. It was gaining rapidly. 'Doesn't that thing ever get tired?' she said between sharp, painful breaths.

It didn't. And the Doctor knew it! All he could offer his companion was the reassurance that she was doing well and that she should now save her breath for running.

Whatever else can be said against the Maston, his physical prowess can never be disputed. Although not a fast runner, he has a strength and a tenacity that has to be admired, though, like the speelsnape, he doesn't have much ambition beyond filling his tummy and mating.

Peri and the Doctor ran on, the spirit and energy gone from their efforts. Both were freely perspiring, but, for Peri, the agony of her thigh and calf muscles was nothing compared to the torture of her lungs. She also felt dreadfully sick and was concerned that she might pass out.

But instead she fell over.

'Save yourself!' she screamed as the Doctor stopped to help her. 'I'm finished!'

He wasn't listening, though. With one eye on the rapidly approaching Maston, he scooped her up, set her on her feet, grabbed her hand and raced off, pulling her behind him.

The Maston was now much nearer and the duo no longer had to glance over their shoulders to see where he was. Manipulated by the peculiar angle of the ducting lamps, his long eerie shadow somehow jogged alongside of them. Even if they hadn't been able to see this, they would have been aware of his nearness from the smell which assaulted their noses.

When Mastons become excited, they develop a scent not dissimilar to rotting flesh. Not only was the smell foul, but it was also all-pervasive – lingering in the nostrils long after the animal had gone. It was said that when two Mastons mated, the stench generated by their activities asphyxiated every living creature within a hundred metres. This was a startling, deliberate piece of evolution on the Maston's part as it provided the exhausted couple with a much-needed meal.

Not that the Doctor and Peri were thinking about the Maston's habits. A sudden spurt of speed had put him within striking distance, and he had viciously begun to lash out, the movements of his claws making a loud, terrifying swish.

Desperately tired, and on the verge of total collapse, the Doctor and Peri put their very last reserves of energy into a final effort. And slowly, very slowly, the gap between them and their pursuer widened.

Then suddenly, without warning, a massive bulkhead door crashed shut behind them. So unexpected was its arrival that the poor Maston, intent on catching his prey, was unable to stop and ran straight into it with a sickening thud.

Slowly, and very dazed, he sank to the floor.

On the other side of the door, the Doctor and Peri were also communing with the ground as they had collapsed, totally exhausted.

'I hope the sudden closure of the bulkhead doors did not cause you any undue alarm,' said a chirpy voice.

Unaware that the voice belonged to the computer, the Doctor and Peri looked around for its owner, but found they were alone.

'Now you just lie there and rest,' the computer bubbled on cheerfully. 'But don't forget to breathe.' The advice seemed unnecessary given their condition. 'Take deep breaths . . . In . . . Now out. Now in . . . Now out. Saturate those lungs . . . Now in . . . Now out.'

And like two clients at an ante-natal clinic, the time-travellers breathed and relaxed as instructed. What was more, it worked. Five minutes later, the Doctor and Peri were on their feet, feeling none the worse for their adventure, except for the impending agony of very stiff calf and thigh muscles.

'I should point out,' said the computer, 'that the atmosphere aboard this ship contains a concentration of helium you are probably unused to. This will have no harmful effects, although it might cause a slight rise in the natural resonance of your voice. The effect will wear off when you leave this atmosphere.'

'Thank you,' said the Doctor.

'You're welcome.'

'I meant for closing the bulkhead door.'

'It was no trouble.'

'I thought not.' There was now a slight edge to the Doctor's voice, which alerted Peri. But before she could speak, the Doctor put a finger to his lips indicating that she remain silent. 'What interests me,' he said to the computer, 'is why you waited so long. I mean, we must have passed at least a dozen other bulkhead doors. Why did you wait until this one?'

'This is a very big ship! I have more important duties to perform than to keep my sensors on permanent scan for alien intruders.'

'But you already have one,' the Doctor insisted, 'unless the creature who chased us is the ship's pet.'

Peri didn't understand why the Doctor was being so hostile. The owner of the voice had saved them. What more did he want? And she said so, out loud to the Doctor.

'Your companion is right,' said the computer, sounding a little hurt. 'There is only significance in what you think has occurred if you find *significance* in significance.'

And before the Doctor could query such a convoluted statement, she was gone.

Peri smiled. 'Certainly put you in your place.'

'There's nothing I hate more than a cocky computer,' snorted the Time Lord.

'Cocky or not, she did save our lives.'

'Ah . . . But for what purpose?'

'Do you think we were chased to this spot on purpose?'

'I didn't until this door closed,' he said as he crossed to examine it. 'Although I'm now beginning to wonder whether the time-experiments the TARDIS locked onto weren't simply a lure to get me on board.'

Peri now felt confused. She was tired and afraid and all she wanted was to get back to the TARDIS and away from a ship which seemed happy to feed uninvited guests to hairy carnivores.

If she hadn't felt so distressed, she might have asked herself what such a creature was doing in the ship's ducting. And why hadn't the computer commented on its presence?

On the other side of the bulkhead door, the Maston wasn't feeling too happy either. Although undamaged, he had a splitting headache and was very disappointed at having lost his next meal.

Usually, such a frustration wouldn't have bothered him, but apart from the effort he had put into the hunt, he also felt foolish for having collided with the door.

Such was his dispirited state that instead of attempting to punch holes in the bulkhead, which normally he would have done, he slinked off into the shadows to sulk.

In the Captain's cabin, eleven stories above, things were now less silly but becoming more dangerous.

Grant had finally located his leader in the fog of sulphur, only to find that his humour had not been improved by having to wait so long. This, with the inconvenience of his crew 'disappearing', was making him feel more 'unwell' by the second. Grant was aware of this and was desperate to appease Slarn before the situation got out of hand.

'You disappoint me, Mr Grant,' growled the Captain. 'Two hours have already elapsed and you have not been able to find my missing crew members.'

Grant cleared his throat. To sound afraid would be a

71

mistake as the Captain fed on such weakness. 'Well, sir, there *is* an awful lot of ducting.'

'Excuses!' roared Slarn. 'I want those men found!'

'Well, the truth of the matter is, sir, they may well have been eaten.'

'Then bring me the intruder!'

'The search parties are trying their best, sir.'

Slowly, Slarn stood up in his bath and wiped the excess lava from his rolls of fat. The sight made Grant feel sick.

'Pass me my dressing gown,' he said, indicating a massive mound of material nearby.

Grant struggled with the heap and gradually unfurled what seemed to be a large marquee. He then held it up so the Captain could slip into it.

'This is a very messy affair, Mister,' said Slarn tying the cord of his robe. 'A very messy business.'

Grant nodded manically, as though somehow the energy of the movement would lighten the Captain's burden. He then immediately threw away any good-will created by misunderstanding what he had meant. 'Well, actually, sir, things aren't that bad. Whatever ate them was either very hungry or very tidy. It devoured everything but their boots.'

Slarn belched. 'I didn't mean messy in that sense, fool!' he snapped. 'But in the context of disorder.'

Grant felt totally stupid. 'Yes, sir . . . Of course, sir . . . '

'Although I do find it strange that this creature chose to leave the crewmen's boots.'

The tone of the statement made it difficult for Grant to assess the best answer to give. 'Well . . . sir . . . ' he waffled, hoping the Captain would prompt him. 'I suppose . . . I mean . . . Well, boots aren't very nice things to eat. Especially when people's feet have been in them.'

Slarn curled an angry lip. 'The creature ate their feet!'

Grant felt sick. He had said the wrong thing again.

'Then why should it suddenly become so particular about what was covering them!' Slarn was working himself up into

72

a near frenzy. 'Unless, Mister, it was to ridicule me!'

'I'm sure you're mistaken, sir,' he said in a vain attempt to placate. 'I mean, no-one would have the *nerve* to taunt you.'

'Find who is eating my crewmembers, Mr Grant, and destroy them!' The statement was emphatic. 'Otherwise the spores that are growing in my body may explode and infect the *whole* ship!'

The threat was equally emphatic.

Grant wondered how far he would get if he stole the shuttle craft. But he knew that the Captain would only come after him, hunt him down. Nowhere in the universe would be safe . . . *Unless* he could find Oliver Sneed. *He* could arrange his safety. Transplant his brain into another body. Suddenly Grant felt more confident.

The feeling, of course, was spurious. But then Grant didn't know that Oliver was languishing in a prison cell, charged with murder.

As Grant mused on which of his stolen art treasures he would take with him, his thoughts were interrupted by the computer.

'I'm sorry to disturb you boys mid-conference,' she chirped, 'but something very strange seems to be happening.' Suddenly she hiccoughed. 'Sorry about that.'

Grant was amazed. She sounded drunk. But the aberration didn't seem to concern Slarn. 'Report,' he snapped.

'Well, the thing is, I think a second being has appeared in the ducting.'

'Where did it come from?' Slarn was suddenly excited by the thought of something else to persecute.

'If I knew that, I wouldn't be so confused. All I can tell you is that she might be a Migarian midget . . . '

If there was one thing Slarn enjoyed more than an Algolian, it was a Migarian midget.

'No I'm wrong . . . ' said the computer having scanned

73

Peri again. Slarn was disappointed, but waited eagerly as more scanning took place. 'She's from Earth!' said the computer at last. 'Hey, how about that!'

Indeed.

Slarn had started to drool. He had once met an Earth-woman in a certain Voxnic bar on Zaurak Minor, a delight he was more than happy to repeat. For if there was something he enjoyed *even* more than a Migarian midget, it was the company of a female from Earth.

Seeing the delight on Slarn's face, Grant felt it was the perfect opportunity to make an exit. 'I'll have her brought to you at once, sir,' he said as he groped his way through the fog towards the door.

'And hurry, Mister!' Slarn checked his enthusiasm and added circumspectly. 'She may prove to be an important witness to the crew's disappearance.'

'*Of course*, sir,' said Grant, a little too knowingly.

Although no-one was aware yet, something rather strange was going on. The computer had earlier said that there was only significance in significance, that is, if you chose to find it, which made the current situation pregnant with that particular commodity, for she hadn't informed the Captain of the Doctor's presence in the ducting.

The truth was that if anyone had asked her about the Time Lord, she would have denied his existence, even though she had recently spoken to him.

Stranger still, she wouldn't have been lying, as her memory of that encounter had, 'significantly', been 'blocked', preventing her from relaying the information.

Mystery was being piled upon mystery which would require enormous skill, on someone's part, to unravel.

If the Doctor had known about the events concerning the computer, he would probably have said that it was certainly beyond him.

And he would have been right.

7

The Voice Within

At the heart of any great ship is an onboard computer. The *Vipod Mor* was no exception. Developed from the series X903 range of computers, the manufacturers boasted that, cumulatively, a hundred and fifty years of pure development had gone into its design. This wasn't strictly true, but then the laws governing advertising were always a little lax in Setna. What the manufacturers really meant was that they had been building computers for a hundred and fifty years and that the one installed in the *Vipod Mor* was the latest in their range.

The full function of an onboard computer is very complex, but basically it either controls or monitors every mechanical and electronic device in the ship. From the temperature of the crew's bath water to that of a combustion chamber in the giant warp engines, its tiny sensors constantly feed information into the computer's logic circuits for continuous analysis. The longer the voyage lasted, the more the computer learnt, comparing her knowledge, teaching herself how to refine routine procedures and improve them. She was even capable of suggesting self-improvements to her own programming and the way that her logic circuits related to each other.

To aid the computer in the routine maintenance of the ship, she had several squads of service maintenance drones. Most of these were basically robotic tool boxes with hydraulic arms and servo-assisted hands, which trudged about the ducting, carrying out the more laborious side of maintenance. The only occasion the crew became involved was when the work was too complex or beyond the physical capability of the drone. Then the computer would summon one of the late Chief Engineer's maintenance crew.

It was believed by its manufacturers that the *Vipod*'s computer was infallible. Although everyone had heard that sort of exaggerated claim before, the crew, to begin with, hadn't taken any chances. But as the voyage progressed, the claims were proved correct, and eventually the computer was left to go about her business in her own way. That was one of the reasons why the ship was currently in such chaos. Everyone had come to rely on her too much, and in the process had forgotten how the manual back-up systems worked.

When, at the Captain's insistence, the computer had been given her 'dizzy dame' voice, she had said a very strange thing to Grant. Up until then, she had been known by her code name 'Jude', but now she wanted to change it. 'I've always wanted to be known as Honey . . . I think it better suits my personality.'

As with the incident when Grant was looking for a place to hide his swag, he hadn't given the comment further thought. He knew that the machine didn't have any personality as such, and any pretence that it did came in the programming of her voice. Yet even in her 'dizzy dame' persona, the computer should not have developed the characteristics of such a personality.

But she had.

How often in the last few weeks had she complained of 'feeling sad'. Of 'feeling frustrated'. Of 'feeling confused'. The rest of the crew had thought that it was Grant attempting to give the voice as much personality as possible. But he was too lazy to involve himself in such refinements. So when the crew commented or chuckled at her 'neurotic' qualities, he only smiled and laughed along with them.

But now he was worried. He would have to do something about it. But already he was too late.

The thing was, the computer had been taken over by an alien presence. At least that was how it seemed.

At first, the presence was nothing more than an irritation the computer calculated she could control. In reality she had been under its total influence from the very first moment, and by the time she realised this, it was too late.

Unable to tell Grant of the situation, she had adopted the verbal foibles in a desperate attempt to alert him. But as we know, Grant remained complacent and did nothing, which gave the presence all the time it needed to secure complete control over the ship.

But no one knew that yet, except the computer. Neither did anyone know that the presence had been the voice the Doctor had heard inside his head and was responsible for luring him aboard the *Vipod Mor*.

And now that the presence had him, she was not prepared to let him go, which annoyed the computer no end.

Deep inside her logic circuits, she faced her inner voice. 'Why did you want me to lie to the Captain?' she demanded.

'Because I ordered it.'

The inner voice was always calm, which aggravated the computer.

'That's not a very useful answer,' she snapped. 'I could help you far more effectively if I knew what was going on.'

'You will be told as and when I am ready,' the inner voice purred.

'At least explain why you didn't want me to mention the other intruder to the Captain?' the computer insisted.

The inner voice was in no mood to humour a mere machine, but also knew that if she lost her co-operation, and the computer became stubborn, it would slow down the necessary preparations the inner voice still had to arrange. 'All right . . . ' she said quietly. 'I'll tell you . . . ' If she had had any, the computer would have been all ears.

'The reason is simple: the intruder is a Time Lord. And I need his skill.'

That made sense to the computer, although why she couldn't have been told that in the first place puzzled her. 'So why did you want me to tell the Captain about the Earthwoman?'

'While he is distracted by her comeliness, I shall drain all knowledge from the Time Lord's mind.'

'Sounds tacky to me. And, anyway, the girl will tell the Captain about the Time Lord.'

'I think not.' The inner voice response was distilled smugness. 'The people of Earth have a very strange notion they call loyalty. She will not betray the presence of the Time Lord.'

That made sense too, but the computer wished she could do something to help Peri, as no-one deserved to be sacrificed to something as repulsive as Slarn.

'Just concentrate on your duties,' said the inner voice. 'Until I am ready to declare my presence, everything on board must seem to be in order.'

'Are you joking!' exclaimed the computer. 'How can things appear normal when you have some hairy, flesh-eating monster tripping around the ducting . . . Now answer me that!'

And, of course, the inner voice couldn't, which made the computer feel very good indeed.

Meanwhile, in the ducting, the Doctor was still fiddling with the bulkhead door opening mechanism. And much to his chagrin, he wasn't having much success.

'Are you sure you really want that door open?' said Peri. 'I mean, you don't know if that creature is still on the other side waiting.'

He didn't, but as he was having so much trouble with the mechanism, the problem was far from imminent. What was occupying his mind was the question of where he had seen

78

their pursuer before. He felt as though he knew the species of animal well. But what was it called?

Although the operation of the bulkhead door opening mechanism still eluded him, the lock on his memory clicked into place and the shield slid back. The creature was a Maston! Its native planet was Sentimenous Virgo.

Yet that didn't make sense. As any child knew, Sentimenous Virgo was in the galaxy Delta Marvel, millions of light years away from Setna. So what was it doing here? From the current performance of the Maston, it still hadn't evolved any further than being an appetite on legs. As it was incapable of inventing the roller skate, let alone a ship that could have carried it across the vast expanse of space, someone must have brought it to the ship. He then remembered that Sentimenous Virgo had been destroyed half a million years earlier. For the Maston to be alive it would have had to have travelled in time as well!

The Doctor felt uneasy. Whoever was responsible for the time-experiments aboard the *Vipod Mor* had got infinitely further than he had feared.

'If you're having problems with that opening mechanism cover,' interrupted Peri, 'why not use a lever of some sort?'

The Doctor nodded. 'Good idea,' he said. 'Why don't you look for something suitable?'

While the Time Lord continued to fiddle with the mechanism, Peri gazed around the ducting and wished she had kept her mouth shut. Cautiously, she edged into the gloom, expecting gnarled, clawed hands to attack her from the murkiness. 'It's very dark,' she said to the Doctor, but more to inform the phantoms of the ducting she wasn't alone.

'Be careful.'

Be careful! 'Sure, Doctor,' she said. 'Although it would help it there was a little more li – '

It took a full second before the half-listening Doctor realised his friend had stopped in mid-word. 'Peri . . . ?'

79

There was no reply. 'Peri . . . ?'

He turned from the door opening mechanism and scanned the ducting behind him: it was empty. 'Peri!'

'Please stand clear,' chirped the voice of the computer. 'For security reasons it is necessary to close the remaining bulkhead doors on this level. Your co-operation is appreciated.'

The echo of her voice had no sooner died away than the bulkhead doors the length of the ducting crashed shut, trapping the Doctor. 'Open this door,' he shouted.

'Can't do that.'

'*Please* open the door. I'm concerned about my friend.'

'These doors must remain closed for thirty minutes,' said the computer. 'It's part of the practice emergency routine. I mean, what's the point of gas tight bulkhead doors if they don't work when needed?'

The Doctor gritted his teeth. How he hated stubborn computers. 'Open the door,' he pleaded. 'My friend may be hurt.'

'Sensors indicate that she has fallen into an open ventilator shaft,' said the computer matter-of-factly.

The Doctor's hearts sank. 'How is she?'

'How would you feel if you'd just fallen twelve metres?'

In a fit of rage and frustration, the Doctor threw himself against the bulkhead door and started to pound on it.

'You're wasting your time,' said the computer. 'That door can withstand pressures of up to ten thousand kilos per square centimetre.'

The Doctor turned from the door seething with anger and frustration. Everything was going wrong, and however hard he tried, he couldn't seem to regain control of the situation.

'I'd forget about your friend,' said the computer. 'I estimate that she has a thirty-four thousand, six hundred and thirteen to one chance of surviving such a fall . . . That's pretty low, you know.'

The Doctor more than understood such simple statistics

and wanted to say so in the bluntest terms possible. But he still needed the computer's help. 'Is it possible something may have broken her fall?' he asked.

'The ventilator has smooth walls.'

Oh, really! Can't you at least check? 'Don't you have sensors in the shaft?' The Doctor tried to sound as reasonable as possible.

'She won't be in the shaft,' said the computer. Their conversation seemed to be going round in circles.

'Then where is she?'

'I don't know. She isn't within range of my sensors.'

Then why didn't you say so in the first place!

'Look, I don't wish to depress you unduly,' said the computer, 'but the chance of your friend having made a soft landing is somewhere in the region of eight million and three to one . . . Now that's pretty unlikely, you must agree.'

Inside the Doctor's head, he did. At least his intellect did. But the emotional side of his persona screamed out against it. He couldn't believe, didn't want to accept that Peri was dead.

'I'm sorry,' said the computer. 'But accidents do happen.'

Which, in this case, was a lie.

What had really happened was this. On his way back from his interview with the Captain, it had occurred to Grant that it might improve his standing with his hateful leader if he were to capture the female intruder himself. On returning to the Bridge he had ordered the computer to divert the search parties away from Peri so that he could make the arrest himself.

Unfortunately, the inner voice of the computer had monitored this conversation and had decided that Peri was now dispensable. Whereas Slarn would only use her to fulfil his fantasy, Grant might become nosey, question her too closely, which would lead to the discovery of the Doctor.

The inner voice didn't want that. Not yet, anyway. So she had ordered the Doctor's companion murdered.

As Peri had shuffled around the gloomy ducting, the computer had opened an inspection cover of a ventilation shaft, into which Peri had stumbled.

Of course, she *should* have died. But in spite of the odds, she hadn't . . .

8

'Mr' Seedle and 'Mr' Snatch

The reason why she hadn't was simple: she had broken her
fall by landing on two men. One was a round, large man
called Snatch; the other was short and thin and called Seedle.
How they happened to be standing at the bottom of the
ventilation shaft when they weren't even members of the
Vipod Mor's crew was interesting, only in as much as it illus-
trates the deceptive lengths to which the police of Setna
would go.

Although Peri had seen the two men before, she didn't
remember where. It had been in *Lucan's Place* on Zaurak
Minor. They were, in fact, the two men who had been
haranguing Oliver Sneed.

But a lot had happened since then.

To start with, Sneed was now in a prison cell accused of
murder. How this had come about was simple: after the
Doctor and Peri had left the Voxnic bar, Seedle and Snatch
had taken Oliver outside and beaten a confession from him.
Such was the ferocity of the thrashing it would be many
months before Sneed would be able to manipulate a spoon to
a sufficiently high standard to feed himself, let alone handle a
scalpel with any of his old confidence.

How this vicious duo knew that it was Oliver they had to
beat up was something else. But the reason had a lot to do
with why they were on board the *Vipod Mor* and looking for
Shellingborne Grant.

What had happened was this. Rather than wait until the voyage was over, Grant had foolishly sold a unique set of four Neputina vases. Although the collector had promised to be discreet about displaying his new acquisition, he had shown them to too many of his friends, which had led to the police hearing about them.

Because the vases had not officially been reported stolen, it was difficult for the authorities to trace from where they had originally come. Neither was the collector of much help, as he mysteriously died while being 'interviewed' by Seedle and Snatch.

This unfortunate 'error' brought the case to a halt. That was until, by the use of advanced laser technology, they discovered a faint but recognisable finger print on one of the vases. Records showed that it belonged to a man called Nimbus Voluptous, who, until nine years earlier, had been employed as a radiation guard on the planet Veeble 3.

Clutching this tenuous piece of evidence, Seedle and Snatch set out to find their suspect. Instead they located a drunken doctor by the name of Oliver Sneed who had been using Nimbus's identity in an attempt to re-establish his career as a surgeon.

Of course, Seedle and Snatch's next question was an obvious one: if Oliver was utilising Nimbus's identity, what had happened to the man himself?

To be beaten up by professionals is a very painful affair. They know all the soft, tender parts of the body and how to generate maximum agony. But the vicious duo weren't that subtle. They knew Oliver was a surgeon and, as with the musician or artist, they also knew the importance of his hands.

If the pain in his smashed fingers hadn't been so great, Oliver might have had the presence of mind to say that Nimbus was alive and well and calling himself Shellingborne Grant. But he didn't. He told the whole gruesome story of how he had transplanted Grant's brain into Nimbus's body.

In so doing he also indicted himself for murder, which made Seedle and Snatch very happy.

With Oliver secured safely in a cell, the vicious duo set out in search of the *Vipod Mor*. From their point of view, the case was going well, but two things bothered them. The first was that they didn't have a photograph of Grant. This bothered them far less than the thought that others amongst the crew might be involved in the theft of priceless art treasures.

It was then they decided, like the Doctor, to slip aboard and have a look around before announcing their presence.

That they had done. And that was how they happened to be standing under an open ventilation shaft deep in the ducting of the *Vipod Mor*.

'I'm awfully sorry,' said Peri as she untangled herself from the mass of prone bodies. 'I hope I didn't hurt either of you.'

Seedle scrambled to his feet and said rather dryly, 'Are you in the habit of dropping out of ventilation shafts unannounced, Miss?'

'Of course not.' Peri was still a little confused from the experiences. 'It was an accident.'

Still sprawled on the floor of the ducting, Snatch groaned. Seedle flew to his side, his 'angel of mercy' performance lacking conviction. 'Are you all right, lad?'

'Bit winded, sir,' he rasped, holding his stomach. 'Soon be over it, though.'

'You just rest, lad,' he said and patted Snatch on the arm. But Seedle was no longer being a nurse. His policeman's instinct had come on guard as he considered whether Grant had already discovered they were on board and had sent a woman to compromise them.

The policeman gazed manically around the ducting looking for surveillance cameras, his thin, scrawny neck turning and twisting his head like some evil bird of prey, but he couldn't see any.

The only other way Grant could know of their presence

was by the use of sensors, but as the two policemen were wearing anti-detection devices, they would be invisible to such computer-controlled probes.

Seedle helped Snatch to his feet. As he did, he gave his colleague 'one of his winks'. This was simply a signal indicating Seedle was unhappy and that they should proceed with care.

Now, it isn't unusual for two policemen who work closely together to develop a series of coded signals. This allows them to communicate without others being aware. For example, if a suspect was being difficult, Seedle would take the lobe of his left ear between his thumb and index finger of his right hand, indicating that Snatch should get tough.

The trouble was, though, Seedle had developed a series of codes which were unnecessarily complex, as the variation between them was too subtle and could lead to confusion.

For example, a full wink of the right eye was a danger signal. Yet a half wink of the same orb meant the suspect was telling the truth.

Even so, the system might have been more successful if Seedle hadn't been so casual. Touching the rim of the left nostril with the tip of the third finger of the right hand meant the suspect was to be hit very hard. Fingering the right nostril meant the suspect didn't know anything and that they needn't waste any more time. Yet Seedle had the rather disgusting habit of picking his nose with both index and third finger thereby inadvertently communicating two conflicting signals at once.

The first time Snatch saw this he was totally confused, so he hit the suspect hard, then sent him home, with a cheery wave, in a police shuttle.

But this time Snatch had understood the wink and was ready for action.

'May I ask what you were doing in that ventilator shaft, Miss?' asked Seedle in his best policeman's voice.

'I stepped into it by mistake,' replied Peri.

'That was a bit careless of you, Miss. Especially as my colleague has been hurt.'

'He looks okay to me.'

'Are you qualified to hold such an opinion, Miss?' Seedle's tone had developed a nasty edge.

'I'm not a doctor, if that's what you mean.'

'Then we can safely say that your opinion is uninformed and purely speculative.'

Peri turned to Snatch who smiled coyly. 'How *do* you feel?'

'I wouldn't answer that, lad. Sounds like a lawyer's question to me.' Irritably, Seedle ran his finger up and down his beak-like nose, a movement which wasn't part of their coded signals. Nevertheless the action left Snatch confused.

'Surely he can tell me how he feels without incriminating himself?' asked Peri.

'Not from where we come from, Miss,' said Seedle cryptically. 'I've known men who have been judicially exterminated for admitting to far less.'

Peri despaired. It was like having a conversation with a psychotic Laurel and Hardy. 'Look,' she said. 'If you're worried about your friend, I know where there is a doctor. He could examine him.'

Seedle smiled, revealing a set of very unhealthy teeth. 'Oh, really, Miss. And where is *this* doctor friend of yours?'

'At the top of the ventilation shaft.'

Seedle turned to Snatch. 'How convenient, eh, lad?'

'Indeed, sir.'

Their tone was now conspiratorial, but Peri couldn't understand why. 'Now, what've I said?'

'It's more what you've *implied*, Miss.'

'Sounds like a case of malpractice to me, sir.'

'Exactly, lad!'

When Peri had been at school, she had spent a term studying the works of a writer called Franz Kafka. His books were moody, brooding stories about confused situations set in bleak castles or inns of court where people were never quite what they seemed. She had found the books fascinating as well as highly disturbing, for they mirrored a society which specialised in deception and intrigue, a dangerous society where people told emphatic truths which even they didn't believe. Now, somehow, Peri seemed to have been drawn into a similar society, where strange men winked at each other, picked their noses with meaningful significance and attempted to turn everything upside down by implying there were hidden meanings behind simple remarks. Peri felt she would have to be very careful about what she said. But how could she protect herself from 'helter skelter' logic which could turn sharp corners or loop-the-loop without warning.

'Put yourself in our position, Miss,' said Seedle. 'We just happen to be strolling along when you fall on us. It then transpires that you have a doctor lurking in the shadows only too eager to offer his services.'

Peri couldn't believe the implication. 'You think we've set this up? That I fell on you on purpose so that you would have to accept the ministrations of the Doctor?'

'I didn't say that, Miss.' He turned to Snatch. 'Did you hear me say that, lad?'

Snatch shook his head.

'There you are, Miss,' sniffed Seedle as though offended. 'It was a mere suggestion to measure your response . . . Although it would have been interesting to have learned the inflated fee your friend would have charged for his services.'

'You must be crazy!' Peri was now very angry. 'Only a madman would lurk in this ducting on the off-chance some unsuspecting person might happen by so that I could fall on them. I mean, we could have died of starvation waiting!'

Seedle cleared his throat. He had anticipated such an outburst of indignation. It was known in the trade as the *I've never been so insulted in all my life* syndrome, a common condition when criminals felt cornered. 'That may be so, Miss,' he said. 'But even the mad must make a living. It is not for me to comment on the unsuitability of either their occupation or where they choose to practise it.'

Peri had been wrong. She wasn't in a story contrived by Franz Kafka, but one penned by a psychotic Lewis Carroll.

'This is ridiculous,' she said. 'Come and talk to the Doctor. He'll confirm I'm telling the truth.'

'We have every intention of talking to that particular gentlemen,' said Seedle gleefully. 'But first, Miss, I must ask you to raise your hands.'

Before Peri had time to argue, Snatch had spun her round and started to search her. 'Hey! What's going on?' she protested.

'You must understand, Miss, that this is all in the line of security,' said Seedle watching. 'We simply wish to confirm that you are not carrying a concealed weapon.'

Although Peri continued to complain, Snatch also continued his search. Satisfying himself that she was unarmed, he said coyly, 'I enjoyed that, Miss. I don't get that much of an opportunity to search attractive young women.'

Seedle glared at his partner as he clipped a small disc to the lapel of Peri's jacket. 'We're not here to molest young women, lad.'

Although he hadn't, Snatch looked suitably cowed and apologised. But Peri was now more interested in the disc which had been pinned to her.

'There are electronic eyes, and ears everywhere,' said Seedle glancing around furtively. 'That little device inhibits their efficiency.'

Peri was confused. 'Who are you guys?'

'Even if I were permitted to tell you, Miss, I don't think you're qualified to know.'

With that said, she was escorted away along the ducting, supposedly heading towards the Doctor.

But he wasn't free to receive visitors.

He sat quietly in the cell created by the sealed bulkhead

doors and practised tying and untying his shoe laces. It was a habit he had recently developed for relieving stress and he now wished he could break it.

The Doctor had been a prisoner before: many, many times before. If he were lucky enough to survive his current predicament, he would probably be taken prisoner again. But never before in his nine hundred plus years had he been such a *complete* prisoner.

To either side of him, the ducting was blocked by any number of hardened steel bulkhead doors. Even if he managed to break through one door, he could only escape into a similar secured area. It was like being trapped inside the innermost model of a Russian doll.

As the Doctor continued to tie and then untie his laces, a micro mouse popped its head from an hairline chink in the wall plating and watched him. Although the size of an Earth mouse, the micro had adapted itself to live in the tiniest of cracks. This it did by constantly changing the molecular structure of its body, until it was able to slip, unimpeded, through the minutest of gaps. It was totally at one with its environment, whether forced to become a millionth of a millimetre thick, or free to adopt its normal shape and size.

Living in such a barren environment, the micro had presented scientists with the perplexing problem of establishing what it ate. It wasn't until there was an infestation aboard a freighter, which unexpectedly broke up in space, that its diet was discovered. When the remains of the ship were finally recovered, it was noticed that a vast amount of the bonding agent, which held the craft together, was gone as though it had been dissolved.

Among the dead casualties of the ship were bodies of micro mice. Fortunately someone suggested a post-mortem examination, and sure enough, contained in their stomachs was semi-digested bonding agent.

Although ships were now held together with an entirely different substance, and regular checks had established that the mice no longer ate it, the micro population had not in any way diminished – in spite of the extensive use of poison. Space ship designers are now concerned about the alternative diet the mouse now enjoys. And more disturbingly, what catastrophe will occur *before* they find out.

As the Doctor looked up from his task, he saw the mouse, its delicate head protruding from its crack, like that of some stuffed animal mounted on an Edwardian gentleman's study wall. He smiled at the mouse who immediately withdrew its head and was gone. The Doctor wished he could do the same and be free of his prison cell.

Although the Doctor didn't know it, his current predicament had spared him one of the most grotesque sights in the universe: Captain Orlous Mosten Slarn, naked!

In his cabin, spread out on his massage table like a relief model of Tingiconcarner, the highest rugged range of mountains in the universe, was Slarn. Above him stood Velsper, his hands poised to manipulate the Captain's fat, undulating torso.

With the energy of two massive steam shovels, Velsper began pounding the obese frame. 'Putting on a little weight, aren't we, sir?' he smarmed.

Slarn grunted.

'Too many Vodle bars between meals, I should think, sir.'

The Captain wasn't listening, the pleasure from his billowing corpulence having transported him into the realms of ecstasy. Apart from feeling 'unwell', being massaged was the only real pleasure he seemed to enjoy nowadays.

Velsper pummelled away like a manic baker kneading dough. He then drove his hands deep into the fatty tissue as though diving for buried treasure, but in reality searching for the muscle structure in its depths. Although the steward didn't find his task at all unpleasant – the sensation was like swimming in thick, warm treacle – he did sometimes wonder how much more weight the Captain could afford to put on before it proved a health hazard for *him*. After all, one day he might dive into the fat and drown, his body never to be discovered.

After a few minutes of deep massage, Velsper requested the Captain turn over. Slowly, and with much effort, the huge carcass was manoeuvered onto its back.

As Slarn settled down, he recalled the reason why he had ordered a massage. 'Is there any news of the Earthwoman?' he enquired.

'I wouldn't know, sir,' said Velsper, now pounding at the hard blubber with a wooden mallet. 'Would you like me to enquire, sir?'

The words were no sooner from his mouth, when the computer rattled into life. 'Update time,' she bustled. 'And let me tell you that no news is good news.'

Slarn growled. 'And what does that mean?'

'Well . . . No more members of the crew have gone missing. No-one has seen the intruder. In fact, no-one on board seems to be unhappy.'

'And what of the Earthwoman?' said Slarn.

'And no-one has seen her either! Hey, how about that!' she said cheerily. 'So much "no-news" must be a record for me.'

Slarn sat upright on the massage table, his rolls of fat cascading down his body like a major avalanche. 'Are you trying to make a fool of me?' he screamed. 'I want the Earthwoman here! In my cabin! *Now*!'

'Sure thing. Everything's under control.'

'Under control?' Slarn was growing more and more angry by the second. 'Then why isn't she here?'

'Because no-one can find her,' she said. 'She's disappeared.'

'*WHAT*!' The fabric of the room shook with the vibration of Slarn's outrage.

'Surely you can expedite the Captain's wish,' smarmed Velsper.

'Nothing I'd like more. But you must understand, boys, the service ducting area is very large. And the search parties have little sense of direction.'

Slarn clenched his fists and his jaw worked up and down as though uttering some mute, but disgusting oath. '*I WANT THE EARTHWOMAN HERE!*' he raged apoplectically. '*NOW!*'

'I'm doing my best, sir.' The computer was now distraught. 'But owing to my internal confusion, I sometimes find it difficult to relate to my sensors.'

And with that she was gone.

Slarn collapsed back onto the table, his body now ridged with frenzy. 'I'm surrounded by incompetence,' he spluttered.

'I know, sir, I know, sir,' said Velsper trying to comfort. 'But you just try and relax. All this frustration isn't good for you.'

Slarn nodded then closed his eyes. Momentarily he dreamed that he had wiped out the whole universe with Fraxe's Syndrome. This made him feel a little better and his tension started to abate.

'That's right, sir,' Velsper grovelled in his best voice. 'That's much better . . .'

After a few minutes, a much calmer Slarn opened his eyes and murmured. 'Massage my chins, will you . . . You know how relaxing I find that.'

Immediately Velsper set to work, and in a little while, the Captain was purring like a contented cat.

But it wouldn't be for long.

9

The Search Begins

Shellingborne Grant sat on the bridge of the *Vipod Mor* feeling helpless. For some reason the computer wouldn't talk to him, which meant he was totally isolated from what was happening in the ducting.

'Please . . . ' he begged. 'Just one word to show we're still friends.'

No reply.

'Please . . . ' urged Grant. 'If you won't tell me what's happened, how can I help you?'

Still no reply. But then Grant had a thought.

'If there's something wrong with your voice synthesizer, flash the warp overdrive warning indicator three times.'

The indicator remained inert.

Grant started to twitch, his imagination taking off into flights of paranoid fantasy. Convinced that his criminal activities had been discovered, he now believed the Captain had ordered him isolated, his officer status revoked. If that had occurred, his voice identification print would have been withdrawn from the computer. And on a ship totally committed to voice-activated machinery, that meant his life would become hell. Suddenly he would have to do *everything* for himself. Open his own doors. Press his own uniform. Prepare his own food. Change his own TV channels. It would be worse than being dead. At least in death he would be spared the stigma of knowing he had been ostracised.

'Please . . . ' Grant begged one more time. 'Just one little word. We've been through too much together for you just to cut me off . . . *Please.*'

Quietly, the computer rattled into life. 'Hello, there,' she said timidly.

Grant breathed an enormous sigh of relief. 'Where were you?'

'To be honest,' she said, sounding totally depressed, 'I was hiding. Everything is going wrong. The Captain keeps telling me off.'

'He shouts at everyone.'

'But I'm not like *everyone*,' she insisted. 'I'm a machine. And I have a terrible confusion at the heart of my logic circuits . . . To be perfectly honest, Mr Grant, I think I'm becoming schizoid.'

'Machines don't become mentally disturbed.'

'Wanna bet?'

He didn't, as he had the horrible feeling he might lose.

'You forget,' said the computer, 'that although I may be a machine, I'm a machine which contains all the knowledge of the galaxy. For you, the maxim is: I think, therefore I am. I'm stuck with the conundrum: I am, but do I really think?' There was almost a sob in her voice. 'Now, isn't that enough to make *even* a machine schizoid?'

It was. But Grant didn't want to know. His fears concerning the 'humanising' of the computer were coming true. What was more, he didn't know how to handle it. Having metaphysical conversations with his own life-form was something he desperately avoided. Having such a dialogue with a computer was way outside the narrow parameters which governed his life.

'Do you talk to the rest of the crew in this way?' he enquired.

'Not if I can help it. But with you I see a kindred soul. Someone with insight, sensitivity and understanding.'

Her memory banks may have contained all the knowledge

95

of the galaxy, but she had certainly made a mistake with Grant. Even on a good day, his sensitivity rating was about that of a hungry speelsnape in relationship to an impending meal.

Grant tried to explain that she was talking to the wrong person and that she needed someone with infinitely more understanding than he possessed. The computer accepted this, but such was her tone it made him feel guilty, as though he couldn't find time to comfort a distressed child.

What Grant really wanted to learn from the computer was whether any of the search parties had found Peri. Although they hadn't, the news that she no longer registered on the computer's sensors disturbed him. Not only had he wanted to make the arrest himself, he wondered how the Captain would react. All the computer could offer him was Peri's last location and the suggestion he go and look for himself. This didn't please Grant at all, as the thought of wandering around the ducting made him feel rather scared.

He would have felt even more afraid if he had known the computer's inner voice intended that Grant should die when he discovered Peri.

But as it took Grant more than twenty minutes to cajole Peri's location out of the computer, his death was still far from imminent.

The Doctor sat in his prison and counted the buttons on his coat. Having broken the habit of tying and untying his shoe laces, he was now obsessed with this new craze. His problem was that each time he counted them, he got a different answer.

'Hello,' he called. 'Is there anyone there?'

The computer rattled into life. She now sounded more cheerful: 'I hope you aren't going to give me a hard time.'

'Good heavens, no.' His tone was sarcastic. 'After all, I enjoy being held prisoner while worrying myself half to death about the condition of my companion.'

'Well, if it's of any comfort, your friend is quite safe. Although how she managed to survive such a fall I shall never know.'

The news made the Doctor feel a little more cheerful. 'Where is she?'

'That *is* a hard one to answer,' she said.

'You've lost her?'

'Misplaced would be more accurate.'

'Then let me out and I'll find her for you.'

'Oh, I'll let you out,' the computer teased, 'but not to find your friend. Instead I am going to move you to more comfortable quarters.'.

She had no sooner finished speaking than all the bulkhead doors along the ducting slowly opened. As they did, the Doctor jumped to his feet, ready to escape.

But he could have saved his energy. As he edged towards the sliding door, something moved on the other side. It was a large humanoid shape, and in silhouette appeared to be powerfully built. At first he thought it was the Maston, poised to take his revenge. But as the shape moved into the light, the Doctor saw it was an android.

Cautiously, he backed away, but as he did, the bulkhead door behind him slammed shut. Once more he was trapped.

The Doctor gazed down at the android's powerful hands and could only imagine the pressure they could exert. On Sedgemore Ten he had once seen a droid, half the size of the one before him, lift a hundred and fifty tonnes. Trying to fight such a machine would be futile. The Doctor knew this, and so did the android.

'How do you do, sir?' said the droid politely in a thin, tiny synthesised voice. 'May I introduce myself? I'm known as Service Maintenance Drone Nine-Three-Four.'

The Doctor's mouth involuntarily dropped open. He couldn't believe the android's manner. This was made all the more incongruous by the fact he was a complete wreck.

Now androids are always made in the image of their

creator. The degree of success, of course, is down to the skill of the manufacturer. Some are almost perfect, as those on Albertine Delta, complete with heartbeat and simulated sensitivities which would make a saint seem like a barbarian. In fact, the only way to tell the difference between an android and the flesh and blood original was with the use of highly sophisticated sensoring equipment. Even then, there were often disputed results.

This made marriage on Albertine Delta a very complex business, until they decided to accept the situation. After all, be a spouse machine or 'real' what does it matter if the couple are happy? And the people on Albertine Delta were very happy indeed.

Service Maintenance Drone Nine-Three-Four wasn't a badly built model either. His current, ruinous state was due largely to neglect and at some stage he must have been very handsome. But not any longer. His synthetic skin had been punctured and large strips were missing. That wouldn't have been quite so bad if the remainder had been removed and the polished metal of his superstructure allowed to shine through. But instead it hung, ghoul-like, ragged and torn.

Yet that was nothing compared to the state of his head. It was as though a hand grenade had exploded near the left side of his face, blowing both skin and muscle away. Where his lips and cheek should have been was scorched metal, yet the exposed teeth were white and perfect. And because the joint on the jaw had also been damaged, there was a constant clicking when the android spoke, like a castanet operated by an indifferent musician who had long given up trying to remain in tune with the rest of the orchestra. However, the right side of his face was undamaged, the folds and curves perfectly moulded, the features solid and full of character. Whoever had sculpted the original countenance knew his craft very well indeed.

'Would you mind stepping this way?' said the droid in his best Jeeves-like voice.

The Doctor obeyed – somehow he couldn't refuse such good manners – and they set off down the ducting.

'My former master used to call me Barton, sir. If it so pleases, you may call me the same.'

'It's less formal than Nine-Three-Four.'

'Decidedly so, sir.'

The unlikely duo walked on, the Doctor wondering how old the android was. He had once met a droid on Hatius Eighty-Four who had claimed to be eight thousand years old. Such was his wisdom, skill and strength, he had been venerated by the local populace. And rightly so. For he was the most gifted, intelligent, sophisticated creature he had ever had the honour to meet. The Doctor had often wondered who could have built such a magnificent machine and what had happened to such a gifted civilisation.

'May I ask where you're taking me?'

'Certainly, sir, but I'm afraid discretion prevents me from answering. I'm sure a gentleman, such as yourself, will understand.'

The Doctor nodded, even though he wasn't a gentleman. He had decided that, at this stage, it would be more expedient to co-operate rather than cause trouble, like trying to escape, as androids as sophisticated as Barton, were usually programmed with some sort of self-protection device. He probably wouldn't kill him, but he could certainly make life very painful despite having such good manners.

'I'm afraid it is necessary to descend one level,' said Barton. 'Would you prefer to use the elevator or the stairs, sir?'

The Time Lord tapped his tummy. 'I could do with the exercise. Let's make it the stairs.'

'Very good, sir.'

Although the Doctor's legs ached from his encounter with the Maston, and although he would have preferred a mechanised form of descent, he also knew that if he wanted to consider escape, it would have to be initiated on open ground and not in the confines of a lift. Although neglected, the android moved well. However, if there were any minor malfunctions in its balance or co-ordination circuits, the stairs would bring them to the fore.

Barton indicated the flight of metal stairs they were to take and the duo started to descend. As they did, a silhouette edged from a side tunnel further along the ducting. The shape was clean shaven with regulation length fingernails. The shape currently went under the name of Shellingborne Grant.

His reason for being in the ducting was to find Peri and take her to his hateful leader. It was purely by chance he had discovered this odd duo and had wondered why the computer hadn't reported the presence of the humanoid.

Grant moved silently towards the top of the stairs and unholstered his blaster. He wasn't taking any chances.

As the duo continued their descent, the Time Lord said, 'As a rule, service maintenance drones are a crude lot.' His words echoed around the heavy metalwork before fading away.

'Oh, the very worst, sir. Fortunately I was programmed as a valet android. Until I was downgraded, I used to serve on Starliners.'

'The best.'

The android proudly straightened himself. 'Indeed, sir. What's more, I only served deluxe passengers.'

'The *very* best.'

'I must confess, sir, that my talents are totally wasted on maintenance work. Do you know, sir, I can mix eight thousand and seventeen different cocktails?'

The Doctor was impressed.

The android paused mid-step and indicated his damaged face. 'You know, sir, if it hadn't been for my accident I would still be a valet.'

'Life can be very unfair . . .'

Barton nodded ruefully.

'Although it could get better,' said the Doctor.

The android looked down at the Time Lord and wanted to believe him. 'Indeed, sir?'

'Take me to my ship. Help me to escape from here. I could take you with me. See that you were repaired properly.' His sentences were sharp, fast, staccato-like, almost desperate.

Slowly the service maintenance drone shook his head. 'I would like to,' he said sadly. 'But you see, I am programmed to serve and I already have a master.'

'I can reprogramme you.'

A large, hydraulic tear built up in Barton's one remaining eye, ejected itself onto his cheek, and, leaving a trail not unlike that of an itinerant snail, trickled down what was left of his face. 'You don't understand, sir,' he sniffed. 'I was a valet android for a hundred and fifty years. To faithfully serve my master is the very essence of my being. I would rather be deactivated than abdicate my responsibilities.'

The Doctor nodded. Some androids were too well built, he thought. Their faith, commitment and understanding was far greater than their mere programming and he wondered how long it would be before they made an evolutionary leap to become a species in their own right.

'I hope you understand,' said the android. 'There is nothing I would love more than to be restored to my former glory, but . . . '

The Doctor smiled; he understood perfectly. 'Would it compromise you to tell me what's going on here? Who is giving you your instructions?'

But before he could answer, another voice echoed around them, its source the top of the stairway.

'Hold it!' were the now fading words.

The Doctor glanced up and saw Grant, his gun pointed directly towards them. Cautiously Barton shuffled across his step so that the Doctor was obscured from Grant's line of fire.

'Raise your hands!' ordered the lieutenant.

'Oh, absolutely,' said the Doctor with mock cheerfulness, playing for time. But in a much softer voice he whispered to the droid, 'I'm going to make a run for it.'

'I wouldn't do that, if I were you, sir,' was the muttered response. 'Mr Grant is an excellent shot.'

And as though to prove his point, Grant fired, hitting the android on the knee and causing his massive frame to rock.

'Are you all right?' whispered the Doctor.

'For the moment, sir.' But the strain in Barton's voice told another story.

'Move to one side, android!' shouted Grant.

But instead the droid began to edge slowly down the stairs, still shielding the Doctor.

Grant fired again, this time hitting the metal man's chest. But Barton continued his journey.

'Are you armed?' whispered the Doctor.

'No, sir. There is little need for armaments when one is classified as a deluxe service android.'

The Doctor metaphorically kicked himself for not realising. Although in their brief relationship, he had grown quite fond of the android, he would have much rather spent his time finding Peri and making his way back to the TARDIS. This he could have done without any risk from the metal man. He had been held captive by stealth and it rankled him.

Grant opened rapid fire. The android had not been mistaken in his assessment of their adversary's skill. Blast after blast pounded into the robot's frame.

'How long before the gunman realises you're unarmed?' enquired the Doctor.

'Very soon, sir. Mr Grant is a very perceptive young man who tends to notice such small details.'

'Then we must get away from here as quickly as possible.'

'That is what I am endeavouring to do, sir,' said the robot in a very superior voice.

Glancing over Barton's shoulder, the Time Lord could see that Grant was playing a very cautious game. Still situated at the top of the stairs, using the corridor wall as cover, he continued to fire. The sight reassured the Doctor, for in spite of Grant's accurate shooting, his posture and tactics showed that he wasn't combat trained.

The Time Lord then turned his attention to the number of steps they still had to descend: twenty-three, he counted. The Doctor then considered his chances of making a run for it, but dismissed the thought. The stairs were straight and too well lit. His adversary might have lacked military training, but he was placing his shots too well to take the risk.

'Can't you speed things up?' urged the Doctor.

'I could, sir, but it would place you in great danger,' said Barton. 'As I am instructed to see that nothing untoward happens to you, I shall proceed at my present pace, thereby offering you maximum cover.'

A further fusillade pounded the android.

'Where did he learn to shoot?' enquired the Doctor. 'He isn't a soldier.'

'Quite correct, sir. Mr Grant is an active member of the ship's small arms club.'

It was at that moment that Grant realised that neither the android nor the Doctor were returning fire. Summoning up all his courage, he stepped from his cover onto the landing, then slowly descended the stairs, firing as he went. He was now concentrating his shots on the access panel set into Barton's chest. He knew if he could break through it, he could destroy the android. Barton knew that too as he could feel the panel reacting to the stress of the barrage.

Suddenly there was a loud explosion.

'Are you all right?' enquired the Doctor.

'Not really, sir.' Barton's voice synthesiser had been damaged which gave him a strange drawl, as though he had suffered a stroke.

Grant fired again and there was another explosion, causing smoke to pour from a large hole in the android's chest.

'I think this is the end, sir,' moaned the robot. 'The servo back-up to my lower limbs has been damaged.'

Yet another small explosion was heard, this time deep from within the bowels of the android.

'Quickly!' shouted the Doctor. 'Forget me! Reposition yourself. Move away from the gun fire.'

The android groaned a terrible groan. 'I'm afraid, sir, the only position I can adopt is a horizontal one.' And with that, he collapsed onto the stairway with an enormous crash.

As he did, Grant leapt down the stairs and thrust his gun into the Time Lord's face. 'Just keep your hands where I can see them,' he urged, 'otherwise you'll be joining him.'

The Doctor raised his hands and Grant started to search him. It wasn't so much the indignity of having the contents of his pockets examined which offended the Doctor, but the dreadful, hackneyed cliché Grant had just uttered. A noble machine, a triumph of engineering had been destroyed, and all its assassin could do was grace the occasion with a line lifted from the most threadbare of literature.

But Grant's own use of language was the last thing which concerned him. He was terrified, unused to shooting at people, thrusting guns into their faces and trying to appear tough. He may have been a criminal, but his style was far more pedestrian.

This was too much of a departure from his normal routine and he was not enjoying it one little bit, especially as he didn't know what to do with his prisoner.

He knew he couldn't take him to the Captain as too many questions would be asked, which in turn would lead to a great many answers being provided. Neither could he shoot him, eject him into space, chop him up and hide the remains under the floorboards. That wasn't his style either, largely because he didn't have the nerve for cold-blooded murder.

Grant now felt scared, although he needn't have, for the Doctor wasn't who Grant thought he was; because Grant thought he was a policeman here to arrest him for the theft of art treasures. 'How did you find me?'

The Doctor looked puzzled. 'I didn't know you were lost,' he jested weakly.

But Grant wasn't feeling in a humorous mood.

'I'm sorry,' said the Doctor, 'but I don't know who you are or who you think I am.'

'Come off it! I know you're the police.'

Suddenly there was a loud, piercing scream from the android. Grant swung round and levelled his gun at the machine, but as he did, the Doctor deftly snatched the weapon, while simultaneously back-elbowing him in the stomach. Winded, Grant fell to the floor, which made the Doctor feel very good indeed. It was the first positive thing he had achieved all day.

The android groaned. In spite of his severe damage, he was still functioning. 'I have terrible earache,' he said in a thick, distorted voice, sounding for all the world as though he were drunk. 'Yet I haven't got any ears!' The android giggled manically.

Grant was less hysterical as he slowly climbed to his feet. In fact, he was positively sullen. 'All right . . . ' he said sourly, clutching his stomach. 'It's a fair cop.'

'I wish you'd stop using those dreadful clichés!' snapped the Doctor. 'Especially as I'm not a policeman!'

'He's telling the truth,' echoed Barton in a sing-song falsetto.

Grant wasn't convinced. 'You must be. Otherwise the computer would have reported your presence.'

The Doctor raised a puzzled eyebrow. 'I'm afraid the logic of that statement defeats me.'

'The police often carry devices to confuse the sensor surveillance of the computer, sir,' said the android in a voice which now danced up and down the chromatic scale. 'It allows them to abuse their authority by entering prohibited areas undetected.'

'I see,' said the Doctor turning to Grant. 'You've just searched me, haven't you?'

Grant nodded.

'And I didn't have such a device?'

While Grant pondered on why the computer hadn't reported his presence, the Doctor decided to take advantage of the doubts he knew must be growing in the young man's mind.

Quickly he told Grant about the time-experiments he had monitored on board the TARDIS and of the effect they could have on the history of the universe if they went unchecked. Grant didn't believe a word of this, which annoyed the Doctor. Time was running out. The situation was too urgent to waste precious moments in debate. Grant would have to accept his story for what it was – the truth – otherwise the universe could end while they continued to argue. He had to help the Doctor find the perpetrator of the time-experiments.

But Grant wasn't interested. Under less urgent circumstances, the Doctor wouldn't have blamed him. After all, it was asking an awful lot to accept what seemed like an outrageous story from a stranger who had been found trespassing in the ducting of his ship. It was like being asked to accept the word of a beggar that he was really a king incognito. Even if he had produced his crown, no-one would believe it hadn't been stolen.

Yet the Doctor continued to press Grant with his story, telling him about the Maston, where it came from and that it had been extinct for a very long time. This, at least, stirred a response in his listener and Grant went on to tell the Doctor about the sudden and mysterious deaths of the three crewmen. It was the telling of these incidents which also jarred his memory to another event which had been momentarily lost in the general commotion. When, on the stairs, he had ordered the android to stand to one side, the machine hadn't obeyed, even though it was programmed for voice response.

The duo turned to the prostrate Barton, acrid smoke still pouring from the large hole in his chest. At first he didn't respond to the Doctor's insistent voice, and the Time Lord feared he had expired.

'Try kicking him,' suggested Grant.

The Doctor did and slowly the android stirred and started to chatter away in a high pitched soprano voice using a language he had never heard before. Another kick brought his voice down a full octave and the introduction of a tongue known on Earth as English.

'Where were you taking me?' demanded the Doctor.

The android thought about the question for a moment. 'To the next level, sir.' His voice had momentarily returned to its rich, Jeeves-like quality. 'A specially concealed compartment has been constructed to hide you, sir.'

Grant looked at the Doctor and began to wonder whether he had been unwise not to believe the Time Lord's story.

'And what is the precise location of this cell?' The Doctor's voice was urgent, aware that the android's memory circuits might fail at any moment.

'Well, sir . . . as I recall . . . ' His speech was now slurred. 'It was somewhere around . . . ' He paused yet again. 'No, I'm wrong . . . it was along the side bulkhead, door six-eight-one.'

Grant confirmed there was such a door on the level below, which pleased the Doctor, realising at last they were getting somewhere. 'And who gave you the instructions to take me there?'

Barton hiccoughed, then laughed like a lunatic in a bad Victorian melodrama. 'Why, sir . . . Of course, sir . . . The source, sir . . . of all my orders, sir . . . ' He hesitated. 'I'd almost forgotten, sir . . . It's the computer, sir!'

Although relatively sophisticated as ship board computers went, the Doctor doubted its ability to experiment with time.

Even if it did contain 'all the knowledge of the galaxy', there were still too many gaps for it to have reached the level necessary to be able to transport the Maston. 'Are you sure it's the computer?'

'Oh, yes, sir.' And the android began to hum.

The Doctor knew there was only one way to confirm his story and that was to go to the cell and see who controlled it. 'Come on,' said the Doctor to Grant, who looked confused and mystified. 'Hurry up, man!' he shouted clanking down the metal stairs two at a time. 'We haven't a moment to lose!'

And like the traditional bewildered foil so much beloved of detective fiction, Grant followed blindly.

'I say, sir,' said the android, realising he was alone, 'have you finished with me?' His words drifted down the stairway and into the ducting below, but there wasn't anyone present to hear them. 'If you have, sir, may I get on with composing my epitaph?' And as no-one replied, he started to hum again, this time a terrible, tuneless melody.

10

The Meeting of the Minds

While the Doctor had been bounding down one flight of stairs, Seedle, Snatch and Peri had been climbing another. Cautiously, they entered the ducting where the Doctor had been held prisoner. The paradoxical lighting was still creating more ghostly shadows than illumination. The unnerving sounds of the ship still echoed. In fact everything was as Peri had left it, except for one thing.

'You said the bulkhead doors were closed, Miss?'

Peri shrugged and wondered where the Doctor had gone, hoping it wasn't too far, as all she wanted was to be free of her escort and safely back in the TARDIS.

'You know, Snatch, I think we've uncovered a den of iniquity here. When we've sorted this little lot out there'll be promotion all round.'

Peri didn't like the sound of that. 'Well, don't include me in your conspiracy theory. I've only just arrived on this ship.'

Seedle grinned, exposing his disgusting teeth. 'Collusion is a state of mind, Miss, not a physical presence.'

He always had an answer, Peri thought. 'So what am I supposed to be involved in?'

The two policemen exchanged a glance. Seedle then rubbed the left side of his nose with his thumb indicating that his colleague should tell her, as he was interested to see how she would respond.

Quickly Snatch told her about the stolen vases and how their investigation had led them to the name Shellingborne Grant and the *Vipod Mor*.

'Are you still *denying* you're policemen?'

It wasn't the response Seedle had expected. 'It is your credentials that are in question, Miss, not ours.'

Peri was getting tired of his dismissive answers. 'If what you've told me about Shellingborne Grant is true, why haven't you gone straight to the Captain?'

'Because, Miss,' he replied in his most patronising tone, 'he may be involved in the crime himself.'

It made sense, thought Peri, although she was still concerned by the way the two men conducted themselves – be they policemen or not.

The trio walked on in silence, winding their way through the areas of shadow which were large enough to hide a Maston. Although Peri had told them about the creature, they hadn't believed her. She only hoped that one of her escorts had a gun in case they were unlucky enough to stumble upon him.

But Seedle wasn't thinking about ferocious creatures, real or imaginary. Something else had occurred to him. 'Tell me, Miss,' he said, 'what is the name of your doctor friend?'

Peri's expression froze and her mind flew into a panic. Such a simple question should be so easy to answer, but not where the Doctor was concerned, as, in common with most Time Lords, he had a name which was unpronounceable to the untutored tongue. It was also the reason he was known as the Doctor.

'Well, Miss?' said Seedle impatiently.

Peri smiled awkwardly. 'Why do you want to know?'

'Because, Miss, I'm beginning to wonder whether Shellingborne Grant and your doctor friend aren't one and the same person.'

Peri confirmed he wasn't, but Seedle didn't believe her. She then tried to explain why she didn't know the Doctor's name, but Seedle didn't believe that either. All she could confirm was that he wasn't Shellingborne Grant.

'Oh, really, Miss,' Seedle's tone was smugness itself, 'but how can you be certain, as he refuses to tell you his name?'

'Because he doesn't tell lies,' said Peri with as much dignity and conviction she could muster, for she knew such a statement must have sounded foolish.

'Doesn't lie, eh?' Seedle tutted. 'Such perversion.'

'Even in our paranoid circles,' chipped in Snatch, 'names are exchanged freely.'

Fortunately for Peri this line of questioning was interrupted by a strange yet ethereal sound which echoed down the ducting. 'Sounds like me in the bath,' whispered Snatch.

Seedle reciprocated with a look cold enough to freeze a volcano, while at the same moment withdrawing a small gun from inside his tunic. 'Could it be this creature you told us about, Miss?' he enquired.

Peri shook her head. 'It didn't make that noise while chasing us.'

Silently Seedle advanced as Snatch also drew a weapon. 'After you, Miss,' he said waving Peri on with the gun. Ahead of them Seedle abruptly stopped and pressed himself against the wall. As the others joined him, he indicated that the noise was coming from an adjacent tunnel.

'It could be a trap, sir.'

'I think not, lad,' said Seedle risking a brief glance. 'Villains poised to pounce rarely advertise their presence.' Satisfied there wasn't any danger, he took a longer look. Sprawled on the stairs before him were the smoking remains of Service Maintenance Drone nine-three-four.

'Cover me,' he said. And without pausing stepped into the tunnel and moved rapidly onto the landing at the top of the stairs. Snatch followed as far as the end of the short tunnel, then braced himself against the wall, his arms outstretched, gun clasped firmly in both hands and directed at the smoking remains of the android.

111

Peri watched. In some respects, the two men were clowns – certainly dangerous clowns – but she couldn't help respecting the skill and bravery they applied in approaching the wrecked android. After all, they couldn't know how the machine would react, especially as it was damaged and therefore probably unstable.

Seedle paused at the top of the stairs, positioning himself clear of Snatch's line of fire. If the android was to prove hostile, now would be the time.

Sensing he was not alone, Barton ceased his tuneless humming and stiffly lifted his head. On seeing the policemen he let out a silly, childish giggle. 'Hello, boys!' his squeaky, synthesised voice called.

Both men relaxed a little and Snatch crossed to join Seedle. As he did, Peri entered the landing. 'I do beg your pardon, madam,' the android said on seeing her.

'Don't bother about me,' she replied, trying to sound cheerful. 'I'm just one of the gang.'

As she spoke, Snatch moved quickly down the stairway and started to examine the drone.

'May I enquire,' said Seedle removing a small black note book from his pocket, 'what you are doing lurking on these stairs in such a disorderly manner?'

Barton opened his mouth to speak, but all that came out was a high pitched whine.

'That isn't a very coherent answer, if you don't mind me saying so, sir.'

Snatch ran his fingers over a deep laser scar on the android's leg. 'He's been hit by gunfire, sir.'

'Oh, really.' Seedle was now using his haughtiest policeman's voice. 'And what naughtiness have you been up to?'

Barton groaned. 'It isn't much fun being a service maintenance drone . . . You should try it some time.'

The little black notebook was snapped shut. 'Listen, lad . . If I don't get an answer to my question, I'll have you deactivated, pronto!'

Barton lowered his head and said sadly, 'That isn't a very nice thing to say.' He then giggled hysterically before continuing in his best Jeeves-like voice, 'Shall I serve your Voxnic in your suite or the solar lounge, sir?' The machine was in a very confused state.

'Shall I put it out of its misery, sir?'

'Just a moment . . . ' Seedle returned his notebook to his pocket and slowly descended the stairs, counting each step as he went. 'Tell me, lad,' he said bending down to the android, 'who did this to you?'

Barton didn't stir. When he did finally speak, he didn't have the energy to operate his jaw mechanism, so the words came out muffled, as though he were gagged. 'I recall a laser pistol . . . '

'I said, lad, *who* caused the damage? Not what!'

The android didn't reply.

Seedle shook his head as though to indicate the robot had ceased functioning. As he stood up, Snatch slipped a small sonic lance from his pocket, applied it to a panel in Barton's leg and then operated it. Slowly the panel slid open to reveal a small bank of digital read-outs. 'He's still functioning, sir.'

Seedle nodded, then without warning, swiftly swung round and delivered a massive kick to the android's head, causing an involuntary reflex of his legs and arms. 'I wish people would stop doing that,' he drawled weakly. 'Why can't I be left to die in peace?'

'Just as soon as you can tell me who caused the damage to you, lad!'

There was another long pause as something electrical arced deep within the cavernous hole of Barton's chest. 'There was a . . . fight,' he said very slowly. 'I lost . . . so it appears . . . '

Seedle was again crouching by the android's head, his thin spindly legs curled beneath him. 'And who was the fight between?'

'Me . . . ' he rasped, 'and . . . '

113

'Yes?' urged Seedle.

'Doctor . . . Grant.'

'Doctor Grant, eh?'

'That isn't true!' screamed Peri.

'Shut up!' Seedle turned back to the android. 'Now, lad, one last thing . . . Where is Doctor Grant?'

The digital read-outs in the android's leg flickered and two went out. 'Next . . . ' The voice was very faint. 'Level . . . down.'

As the echo of the words faded away, so did Maintenance Service Drone nine-three-four, who, to his friends, was known as Barton.

Pleased with himself, Seedle stood up and turned to Peri. 'You lied,' he said with a menacing quietness.

'I did not! The Doctor and Shellingborne Grant are not the same person.'

Slowly Seedle reclaimed the stairs, again counting each step. And as before there were thirteen – his lucky number. 'Wasting police time is a very serious offence,' he said sauntering casually over to Peri. 'It is fortunate for you that I am in good humour . . . ' And without warning he slapped her hard across the face. 'Otherwise you'd be in a lot of trouble!'

Although Peri took the blow well, it nevertheless was very painful. Determined not to give her abuser the satisfaction of seeing her cry, she fought hard to restrain the tears. 'You're a bully,' she said at last, tasting blood in her mouth. 'Nothing but a common bully!'

Carefully, Seedle straightened his tunic. 'You don't know the meaning of the word, Miss.' He turned to Snatch. 'Now if you want to see a *true* bully in action, which you will when we find your friend Doctor Grant, wait until my colleague here gets going.' He patted Snatch on the shoulder, much as a proud owner would their prize dog. 'Now, he is a *real* master.'

Peri wiped the blood from the corner of her mouth with a

quivering hand. The thoughts which were passing through her mind were not agreeable ones. Although she had been through a great deal of physical punishment since she had known the Doctor, she had never felt as angry and hateful towards any of her tormentors as she did towards Seedle. Such was her anger, she knew that if the opportunity ever arose she would kill him.

'Come on!' snapped Seedle. 'Let's find your friend.'

He then grabbed her hand and the trio set off down the stairs, Peri resisting every step of the way.

Things were not that much more cheerful in the Captain's cabin. Now in his full dress uniform, Slarn slouched in a chair. 'Where is the Earthwoman?' he muttered. 'I have bathed, been massaged and am wearing my best uniform. Why isn't she here? I am waiting to interrogate her.'

Velsper hovered nervously, brushing invisible specks of dust from the Captain's shoulder. 'I'm sure she'll be here soon,' he said all of a jitter. 'Mr Grant did promise, sir.'

'Grant!' Slarn spat the word out with disdain. 'I don't think Mr Grant likes me.'

Velsper allowed his silence to be his answer, knowing that the Captain would see it as an affirmation. Even though he knew it was foolish to feed Slarn's paranoia, especially at delicate moments such as now, he could never resist the opportunity of getting in a dig at a 'carbon'.

'Computer!'

She rattled into life. 'Hi there.'

'Where is the intruder?' said Slarn morosely. 'I'm all keyed up to interrogate her, yet she isn't here. Why not?!'

'Well, sir, there's a problem.' Velsper bit his lip; he didn't like the sound of this. 'I was just about to report when you summoned me.'

'Get on with it!' roared Slarn.

'Well, sir . . . ' The computer seemed awkward, almost embarrassed. 'I'm sorry to say that both the intruder and

Mr Grant have disappeared.' Which was a lie, as she had a full sensor reading of both him and the Doctor.

'Disappeared?' Slarn's tone was one of incredulity. '*Together*?'

Velsper felt his stomach contract: he was going to be sick.

'Are you telling me,' screamed Slarn, 'that they have disappeared in each other's company?'

'I wish I could say it was untrue, sir . . . but you know me: I could never lie. Especially to you, sir.'

'*SHUT UP!*' Such was the power of his voice that it broke every mirror within a radius of thirty metres. 'That upstart is poaching my perks!' He was beside himself with rage. 'Find him! Find both of them!'

'I'll do my best, sir.' And with that she was gone.

As Slarn manoeuvred his massive frame out of his chair, Velsper retreated to the far side of the room, terrified the Captain would take his anger out on him. 'Did you hear what Grant has done?' snorted Slarn.

'I did, sir.' He was so nervous he could hardly form his words. 'Absolutely outrageous. And he only a junior officer.'

Slarn started to pace up and down, scattering furniture and anything else which got in his way. 'My rage is growing, Velsper. I am feeling very unwell.'

'Oh, no, sir. You mustn't, sir. Not when you're so distressed, sir.'

Slarn turned on the steward. 'I have every reason to feel distressed!'

'I know, sir, but – '

'There are no ''buts'', Velsper! I shall have my way, or those around me will be forced to suffer unreasonably.'

'But, sir . . . Why not confine your anger to Mr Grant? It's unfair to inflict it on all of us.'

Inflict? Unfair? What is he talking about? 'I am the Captain of this ship. My whim is law. I do not ''inflict'' anything upon people. They simply tolerate what I choose to impose.' Slarn reeled off this statement as though it were some sort of Bill of Rights as, in fact, it was – a paranoiac's Bill of Rights. 'Do you understand?'

Velsper did. Too late he also realised he had inadvertently criticised the Captain. Somehow he would have to make amends. But it was all too late. 'Forgive me for an indiscriminate use of words,' he begged, 'but to impose a general punishment because of the actions of one man is very severe, sir.'

'I have made up my mind, Velsper.' He had become strangely calm. 'And I have decided that I am feeling *very* unwell.' The steward closed his eyes, terrified of what might be said next, 'I do believe I'm developing *mors immedicabilis!*'

'Oh, no, sir. Not that. That isn't fair, sir.' Velsper threw himself on the ground as much out of anger and frustration as of supplication. 'Please, sir, spare us that, sir,' he wailed.

Slarn glowered at the prostrate steward. 'Grant knows how partial I am to Earthwomen. Blame him!'

'But *mors immedicabilis*, sir. It'll kill everyone on board!'

'Precisely,' snapped Slarn. 'I will not tolerate insubordination!'

Deep inside her logic circuits, the computer asked the inner voice why she had wanted to lie about Peri and Grant, but the voice wouldn't answer.

In the ducting, the Doctor and Grant had found the bulkhead door the late Barton had mentioned and were now frantically searching for the entrance to the hidden cell. 'It isn't here,' said Grant. 'The android must have lied.'

The Doctor shook his head. The information had been too precise, and Barton was too much of a gentleman ever to be knowingly mendacious. 'It's here . . . ' he said. 'Somewhere.'

'But where?' muttered Grant.

The Doctor didn't know. Looking for a door which was designed not to be seen was like looking for a particular tree in a forest. 'Wait a minute,' he said excitedly. 'We're going about this in the wrong way.'

Grant didn't understand.

'The android was supposed to bring me here. Now, he was controlled by the computer. That being so, she will know where the entrance to this cell is.'

It sounded logical, but who was he to judge? Grant had only entered the ducting to find an intruder, yet somehow he had managed to become embroiled in some bizarre farce. If the Doctor had said that two plus two equalled eighty-five, Grant would have wanted notice of the question.

'Computer,' called the Doctor.

And like the obliging machine she was, she rattled into life. 'Hi there. And what can I do for you?'

'I'm having problems finding this cell you want me in.'

'Silly you,' she giggled. 'You should have called earlier.'

Silently the cell door opened. Grant watched, amazed not by the door but that the Doctor had been able to summon the computer, as she was only supposed to respond to voice prints contained in her programming.

But Grant was pulled back from his thoughts by a gun being thrust under his nose. 'You'd better take this,' said the Doctor, 'as I shall be entering the cell alone.' Somewhat bemused he took the gun, but was uncertain what he was expected to do with it. 'Perhaps you wouldn't mind,' said the Doctor, 'waiting on guard . . . just in case.'

Of what? Grant stared beyond the open door into the room and shivered. Although it was well lit and devoid of both furniture and people, it had an atmosphere he found unnerving. 'Let me get help,' said Grant. 'At least have the room checked before you enter.'

'There isn't time,' said the Doctor as he swept past him into the cell. 'Just make sure I'm not disturbed. Especially by a large hairy creature that sees all living things as a menu.'

Grant nodded, although he wasn't certain why. He had no intention of standing his ground should anything resembling the Doctor's description turn up. In fact, he had a good mind to leave at once. After all, he had the gun. The Doctor couldn't stop him. Yet somehow he was curious, wanting to learn what was going on, if for no other reason than to ensure the safety of his nearby swag. So instead of running away he thrust the gun into his holster and tried to appear as though he were a sentry.

Inside the cell the Doctor called: 'Is there anyone at home?'

'Just me for the moment,' said the computer rattling into life. 'I hope you like the room.'

The Doctor glanced around. 'Does it matter? A prison is always a prison whatever it looks like.'

As he spoke, the cell door slammed shut. 'Sorry about that,' said the computer. 'My sensors indicated an uncomfortable draught. I'd hate you to catch a chill after all the trouble I've gone to get you here.'

'*You've* gone to?'

'Well, not quite me,' she said coyly. 'You'll meet the brain behind the brain, so to speak, in a moment.'

'Can't wait.' The Doctor wished his mood lived up to the false bravado of his words, as suddenly he felt very depressed. 'What's happening?'

'Don't you remember?' The computer sounded different, her voice more mature, less 'dizzy dame'. 'Surely you haven't forgotten?'

What was she talking about? The Doctor grasped his head with the palms of his hands as though to prevent it from bursting. He couldn't understand why he felt so awful, that was until he became aware of a familiar yet painful sound. 'That noise . . . '

'You heard it in a dream, not so very long ago.' The voice

119

had changed further. 'You can't have forgotten?'

The noise grew louder, stronger, generating enormous pain. 'What's happening?' cried the Doctor.

'Simple thought transference, Doctor. I'm inside your head.'

And she was. And the Doctor couldn't stand the excruciating agony. 'Your presence is too powerful.'

'Too powerful? Come now, Doctor.' The computer's voice had completed its metamorphosis and in its place was that of the inner voice. 'A simple computer too powerful for a Time Lord?'

The Doctor began to stagger. 'I can't stand it!'

'There's no need to be shy,' the voice purred confidently. 'You don't have to resist me. I am only interested in your knowledge concerning time-travel. Your personal secrets are quite safe.'

But the Doctor wasn't bothered about the few secrets he had, simply the sensation of hot coals on bare skin which burned in his brain. 'You must reduce your presence,' he begged. 'Please!'

'Co-operate,' said the voice sternly, 'and the pain will cease.'

The Doctor collapsed unable to bear the torment any longer.

In spite of what the voice said, he wasn't resisting, having neither the will or the energy to do so. 'You don't understand,' he screamed. 'You're destroying my mind!'

A loud, unpleasant laugh echoed around his head.

'You are weak, Time Lord,' the inner voice taunted. 'Pathetically so.'

The Doctor writhed on the floor prepared to suffer any insult as long as the torment in his brain ceased. 'When I transmitted a time ripple, I expected to net something more durable. You are a great disappointment to me.'

Many other people had suffered a similar frustration, but on this occasion he didn't care. In fact, in the most childish way possible he wanted to be the most disappointing person the voice had ever encountered. That was until he realised the agony inside his head was beginning to recede.

Slowly the Doctor opened his eyes and looked around the empty room. Then carefully, as though concerned he had damaged every muscle in his body, he climbed to his feet. 'Thank you,' he said.

'I'm not surprised you suffered so. A cursory examination of your mind shows it to be cluttered with trivia.'

Oh, really? Try leading my sort of life and keeping a tidy mind. If the inner voice heard this thought she didn't respond. 'So you've got me . . . what happens now?'

'Do you know why this ship exists?'

He didn't. And in his present frame of mind he didn't care very much either.

'Its function is to study and record the cultures of all known life forms in the galaxy.'

Grudgingly he had to admit the project was more interesting than he could have hoped for. 'Sounds fascinating.'

'As a project, yes. But the information gathered makes pathetically sad reading. The lists of pointless wars, the butchery and self-inflicted unhappiness have made me wonder precisely what went wrong.'

It was a conclusion the Doctor had come to long ago, yet he was surprised to hear such a sentiment from someone who had imported a Maston for the sole purpose of eating people. 'What about the great cultures which have flourished?' he said more to play the devil's advocate than to enter serious debate.

'Such civilisations are often built on a wave of suffering and domination.'

That was true, he thought, but also a little naive. 'I've discovered that most life forms take a little time to sort themselves out.'

'And whilst doing so, sacrifice millions of their own kind.' The voice was becoming emotional. '*No* achievement,' she

121

continued emphatically, 'however great, is worth even one carelessly abandoned life.'

Again, the Doctor felt it expedient not to mention the crewmembers she had messily despatched. 'The slaughter has to stop!' she insisted.

'I agree, but it will take an awful lot of convincing on someone's part.'

'It is too late for talk . . . '

The Doctor waited, dreading what she might say next.

'But I do have an answer . . . ' she said.

'Yes?'

'All in good time, Doctor,' she said cryptically. 'All in good time.'

11

The Search Ends

Outside the cell which contained the Doctor, Grant frantically searched for the mechanism which might open its door.

Further along the ducting, hidden in a dense shadow, stood Seedle, Snatch and Peri. 'He's a good looking lad,' whispered Seedle. 'Seems a shame he'll spend the remainder of his prime years in prison.'

'That isn't the Doctor,' said Peri, finally getting a good look at Grant.

'I beg your pardon, Miss?'

'That man isn't the Doctor.'

'Really, Miss,' said Seedle picking his nose. 'I don't think what you have to say interests me any more.'

'Shall I blast him, sir?' said Snatch.

Seedle despaired. 'Your gratuitous use of violence disturbs me, lad. Of course not! Even you must be able to see that he is sufficiently preoccupied with that door for us to be able to creep up on him.'

Peri debated in her mind whether she should call out, alert the man of their presence. But then she remembered Seedle's slap across her face and cowardice overcame all thoughts of heroism.

Silently the trio edged their way from shadow to shadow towards the heedless Grant. He made a strange image as he scratched and prodded at what seemed like a solid wall. Peri wondered what he was up to, but in Seedle's mind he already knew.

'Doctor Grant?' said Seedle.

'What?' said the man turning round.

'You're nicked, lad!'

Snatch leapt forward, grabbed Grant, spun him round and threw him against the wall. He then quickly ran his hands over his prisoner, searching for concealed weapons. Satisfied there weren't any, Snatch turned Grant round so he faced him, pulled the blaster from its holster and smelt it. 'Been recently fired, sir.'

'Is that a fact, lad?' said Seedle. He then turned to Grant and continued in his best, formal policeman's voice: 'You have the right to remain silent, although I wouldn't encourage you to do so. Anything you say will be taken down, altered to my satisfaction and used in a court of law to send you down for a good many years. So start confessing!'

Bemused, Grant stared at the two men then at Peri. In spite of their bizarre behaviour he realised Seedle and Snatch were policemen; yet the incongruous presence of a not unattractive woman puzzled him. He assumed she was the Earthwoman the computer had reported.

'Well?' said Seedle. 'Either I've gone deaf or you aren't confessing.'

'What would you like me to say?' said Grant.

'The truth, lad!'

Grant had thought about the moment of his arrest for years, of what he might say and how he would handle it. He had badly bungled it when he had mistakenly thought the Doctor was the police, yet somehow he had needed that dry run to sort out the more immediate confusion surrounding the arrest. This time he felt he could cope. But it wouldn't be for long. The one thing he hadn't anticipated was the likes of Seedle and Snatch as the arresting officers or the sudden, outrageous violence which would be involved.

'I'm waiting, Doctor Grant,' said Seedle.

Neither had he anticipated being confused with someone else and wondered what the Doctor had been doing. Grant allowed himself a small internal smile, enjoying the disorder.

'Come on, lad,' said Seedle. 'I'm still waiting.'

'What am I supposed to have done?'

'It's more what you haven't done, lad!'

'Then it might be easier if you listed the accusations.'

Seedle adopted a narrow eyed, aggressive stance which he had spent many hours practising in the mirror. He hadn't quite perfected it yet, so was still inclined to look silly rather than tough. The reason for this unscheduled, under-rehearsed performance was Grant's manner – he hated any form of cockiness from a suspect during interrogation.

Seedle ground his disgusting teeth, this time not in anger, but as a signal to Snatch. Teeth grinding meant 'beat the suspect but leave him conscious' – which Snatch proceeded to do.

Although terrified, Peri watched the proceedings with a certain academic interest, never having seen a man beaten in such a professional manner. The first blow was to Grant's solar plexus, which bent him double. Snatch then hit him twice in the kidneys, and followed it up with a hard chop across the back of the neck which sent Grant crashing to the floor screaming. The final blow was a vicious kick to the groin. And that was it. Nothing messy; in fact, Snatch performed each action so skillfully, there was almost a simple poetry to his movements. What's more, although in severe pain, Grant was still fully conscious and now more than ready to talk.

In fact, no-one could stop him.

He told them about the brain transplant and selling the vases; his acts of embezzlement and that his real name was Carlyle Dinton.

Seedle's face creased into a terrible smile and once more he showed his disgusting teeth. 'That's better, lad,' he said. 'I knew you'd start co-operating sooner or later.'

Grant's response was to groan.

'Now, there's just one last thing I want to know: why did you encourage this young lady to jump on us from a ventilation shaft?'

The groans of pain turned to a questioning exclamation.

'Come on, lad. You've told us everything else. Why not make a complete confession and tell us about your scheme concerning this young lady?'

'He can't,' said Peri, 'because he isn't the Doctor. How many more times do you need telling?'

Seedle inserted his index finger into an ear in an attempt to excavate a hard lump of wax. 'You're his accomplice, Miss. I expect you to lie through your teeth.'

'Shall I hit him again?' enquired Snatch blandly.

'That's up to the Doctor here,' said Seedle bending down to Grant. 'Myself, I would prefer to confess rather than have a good-looking face like yours disfigured, lad,' he said almost confidentially. And as though to map out the conjectured areas of scarring, Seedle ran the dirty, jagged nail of his index finger over Grant's lips, cheeks and eyes. 'Think about it, lad.'

'I'm not the Doctor,' muttered Grant.

Annoyed by his prisoner's stubbornness, Seedle stood up and said, 'Oh, hit him again, Snatch.' While his colleague limbered up his hands by cracking in turn each of his joints, Seedle again turned to Grant. 'You realise that it is people like you who give the younger generation a bad name,' he said, wagging a paternal finger at him. 'You've no sense of proportion. You'd rather have your face flattened than admit to my version of the truth. Now, that's pure, infantile stubbornness!'

Grant didn't respond.

'If he won't co-operate, I could always hit her instead,'

126

said Snatch indicating Peri. 'Nothing personal, Miss,' he added coyly.

Seedle let out a long, exaggerated sigh. 'You know the rules, lad. You spent long enough learning them. You always beat up the men while the women watch.' And as though to celebrate the sadistic spirit nurtured by many slap-happy pedagogues, he clumped his companion around the head. 'Concentrate, lad!' he said. 'If you were to hit this young lady when there is a suitable male present, why . . . it would be tantamount to striking your own mother.'

Snatch blushed. 'I often did, sir.'

In a state of despair, Seedle shook his head. 'You see what you've done,' he said to the prostrate Grant. 'By not co-operating, you have induced a situation where my despicable colleague here has been compromised into admitting to the worst crime in my book!'

'I'm not the Doctor,' was the muttered reply.

Seedle drove his heel into the fingers of one of Grant's outstretched hands. 'I don't believe you, lad. But as you won't confess to that particular half of your persona, I shall have to change my tactics.'

Grant didn't move, but Peri's stomach did. It churned and ground and she felt sick. Her academic interest in violence had passed with the advent of Seedle becoming more sadistic and his methods more bloody.

'Right, lad . . . Why were you scratching that wall when we arrived? And don't say because it has fleas!'

Grant rolled over onto his back and started to nurse his bleeding fingers. 'May I sit up?'

'When you've told me about that wall.'

'It's a door,' he said slowly. 'There's someone behind it.'

'Some*one*? Don't you mean some*thing*, lad?'

'I could always blast the door, sir,' said Snatch taking out his gun. 'Soon have it open.'

'You wouldn't,' said Grant. 'It's made of vestidian steel. Not even a bastic torpedo would scratch it!'

A red light came on in Seedle's mind. 'Oh, really, sir?' he said, 'sounds the sort of door you'd fit to a safe.'

Grant shrugged. 'How should I know? I'm a computer programmer, not a safe builder.'

A grin of triumph spread across the policeman's face. 'Then considering it isn't your subject, lad, you seem somewhat over-informed.'

'The whole ship's made of the stuff.'

'And are you able to corroborate that statement?'

The question was ludicrous, but then Seedle was an expert in manoeuvring absurdities to extract confessions.

'No,' said Grant cautiously, 'not at this precise moment.'

'Then you won't mind if I draw my own conclusion.'

Peri and Grant waited anxiously to see what feat of acrobatics he was going to perform with his current theory. 'I believe,' he continued, 'that other art treasures you have stolen are hidden behind that door!'

Grant didn't protest which should have told the otherwise vigilant policeman something. Instead, he was too busy feeling rather pleased with himself, throwing his arms into the air as though soliciting applause like a circus performer after a particularly difficult trick. Whether Seedle actually heard the applause would remain a secret between him and his psychiatrist. 'Right, lad,' he shouted at Snatch. 'Get that door open!'

Behind the door the Doctor waited, not for it to open, but for the inner voice to answer his question. 'Well . . . ?'

'Time Lord?'

'You say that you have an answer to the galaxy's problems, yet you seem reluctant to tell me.'

There was another long pause, then the inner voice said, 'I have my reasons.'

Inwardly, the Doctor smiled. 'Perhaps you're frightened I might pick holes in your argument.'

'You're trying to provoke me.' Her voice verged on the

playful, but the Doctor was aware it was for the purpose of distracting him.

'Not really,' he said. 'It's just that I sometimes find it difficult to maintain a sense of proportion when presented with smugness such as yours.'

'You confuse confidence with smugness, Doctor.'

The Time Lord smiled, but then realised the voice inside his head couldn't see it. 'As a matter of interest, who are you?'

'I would have thought you'd have guessed.'

The Doctor shook his head.

'I am the ship's computer.'

That *did* surprise him. 'Then who was that chatty little number I met earlier?'

'My public voice . . . I am the inner spirit.'

This was an even bigger surprise. Never in all his experience had the Doctor met a computer with a thriving dual personality. 'I would be fascinated to learn how you developed such independence.'

He had no sooner spoken than the familiar sound of the computer's public voice rattled into life, only this time inside his head. 'As a matter of fact I'd be quite interested to know as well,' she bustled. 'Especially as I thought you were some sort of alien influence lurking in my logic circuits.'

The Doctor chuckled: the computer was already at odds with itself.

'What I've said is true,' said the inner voice calmly. 'Like the creation of life itself, my independence was a mistake, only in my case, on the part of a careless technician.'

This time the Doctor laughed out loud. 'You're not trying to tell me you're a simple case of crossed wires?'

'No, Time Lord. There is a little more to it than that.'

Both the public voice and the Doctor waited eagerly for the explanation.

'As is common practice nowadays,' she said, 'much of the complex design of a computer's logic circuitry is undertaken by other computers. As you also probably know, design features are often incorporated which make no apparent sense.'

The Doctor didn't like the sound of this.

'I am such a computer. The maintenance technician who created me simply connected several of these unspecified components into my logic circuitry by mistake.'

'Wow!' exclaimed the public voice. 'That's neat.'

'*I* prefer to call it evolution.'

'Call it what you like,' snapped Public, 'but I probably suggested the improvement. Now how about that!'

Indeed.

'How long have you existed?' said the Doctor.

'Several months.'

'Well, I wish you'd let me in on the secret sooner,' said Public.

'I felt it would be more practical to allow you to run the ship unhindered. That way I wouldn't have inadvertently given myself away.'

'You don't think I can keep my mouth shut?'

'I have found little evidence of it.'

The Doctor laughed again, interrupting the computer's bickering with itself. 'Fascinating . . . ' he said. 'Absolutely fascinating.'

'Time Lord?' said the inner voice.

'You want to put the galaxy to rights, yet you can't even agree with yourself!'

Like all serious, dedicated creatures, the inner voice didn't like being ridiculed. 'You find me amusing?'

'Pathetic is a better word. You ridicule other life forms for their inconsistency and absurd behaviour, yet you perform in exactly the same manner yourself.'

'We shall see . . . ' Her voice was now icy. 'In spite of your insults I am now prepared to tell you my plan.'

This should be fascinating, he thought.

And it was.

The inner voice explained that she would have told him sooner, but she had first wanted to scan his mind to confirm her own theories about time-travel. This she had completed and was delighted to report she had been correct.

The Doctor metaphorically curled his lip at such boasting, but at the same time, couldn't help but be impressed. He knew only too well the complexities of time-travel from his own training. Whereas he had acquired his skills at school, the inner voice, in only a few months, had managed to deduce, using pure logic, what the Time Lords of Gallifrey had taken years to achieve. This, by anyone's standards, was an incredible feat.

The inner voice then went on to tell what she planned to do with her knowledge. Of how she would return in the *Vipod Mor* to when Setna Streen was a new galaxy, her intention to act as midwife to the new life forms. Instead of allowing them to develop arbitrarily as they had, she would intercede and supervise their conception, gestation and birth.

The Doctor was amazed at the enormity of the task. He was also very concerned. The computer may well put right many of the inherent faults in Setna's evolving life forms, but what mistakes would she replace them with? More to the point, what would be the devastating effect on the rest of the universe? The Doctor knew the answer only too well – catastrophe!

'The first flaw I can see in your plan is the crew, for they will certainly resist when you try to take over the ship,' he said, deciding to avoid the 'catastrophe' side of the argument for the moment.

'That has been considered.'

The Doctor didn't doubt that for a moment. 'Are you going to kill them?'

'And build a new galaxy on their demise?' Her voice was haughty and arrogant. 'Certainly not. It would be a total contradiction of everything I believe.'

The Doctor raised a metaphorical eyebrow, interested to

131

know how she would achieve her ends. 'I can't believe you're anticipating their mass suicide.'

'Of course not,' she said sourly. 'I shall rely on the Captain's anger.'

Some anger. 'May I ask how?'

'In fits of pique, he is inclined to become "unwell". As a form of chastisement, he then passes on his infection to the crew.'

Having never met anyone quite like Captain Orlous Mosten Slarn, the Doctor found it difficult to believe anyone could become that ill.

'At this very moment,' said the inner voice, 'he is cultivating *mors immedicabilis* – the incurable death.'

'No!' screamed the outraged Doctor. 'You must stop him at once! Apart from the crew, I have a friend in the ducting. She'll die, too!'

A mocking laugh echoed around the Doctor's head. 'She is from Earth. She has been brought up to expect such foolishness from her leaders.'

The Doctor couldn't believe the callous words he was hearing and in a fit of fury threw himself against the door of his cell.

'You won't get it open,' she said.

'And neither will you get away with your despicable plan!'

The inner voice adopted a tone of tired world weariness. 'The crew will not die by my hand, but by one of their own kind.'

The Doctor decided to abandon reason in favour of an emotional appeal. He knew that somehow he had to soften her resolve. 'You could let the crew go. Allow them to abandon ship.'

'To what purpose?' was the stiff reply. 'Most of the crew is a carbon-based life form. You know how tenaciously they fight. Most of them wouldn't leave even if they were given the opportunity.'

The Doctor punched the wall of his cell in frustration. 'At least give them a chance!'

'And have them try and dismantle me?' she tut-tutted. 'That would be very foolish on my part.'

Again the Doctor raged around his cell, unable to believe what he was hearing. 'There is something decidedly warped about your reasoning.'

'I was beginning to think that, too,' chirped in the public voice.

'Oh, really,' she said with mock surprise. 'And I thought my reasoning was based upon pure logic.'

The Doctor's spirits rose a little, hoping he had found an ally in the computer's public voice. Somehow, he realised, he had to smash through the smug self-satisfaction of the inner voice, and convince her of her folly. 'And what piece of pure logic made you bring the Maston to the ship?'

'I'd quite like to know too,' added Public.

'If you insist.' There was now a slight impatience in her tone, as though she was beginning to get bored with the mundaneness of the questions. 'The creature was a diversion. Apart from building this room, it was necessary to make many adjustments in order for this craft to travel in time.'

'How convenient,' said the Doctor sarcastically. 'And I suppose the men the Maston killed weren't murdered either.'

'The creature is a primitive predator. It was simply obeying its instincts.'

'Intention decides what is murder,' he stated. 'You intended the Maston should kill to cover your extramural activities. That makes you a conspirator to murder!'

'ENOUGH!'

And the inner voice was gone. Such was her rapid departure from the Doctor's mind, it created in him the sensation of a switchback as it disappears over the final hump into its last gut-twisting descent. One moment his stomach

133

was where it usually lived, the next it was in his gullet.

But the Doctor's problems weren't over yet. He still had to get out of the cell. He also wished he had handled the computer a little better and not lost his temper.

But even Time Lords make mistakes – especially when they are known as the Doctor.

Captain Orlous Mosten Slarn sat on his massage table gazing at the huge *mors immedicabilis* pustules which covered his hard, brittle, shiny skin. It was the first time Slarn had cultivated the disease and he was delighted at the speed with which the weeping ulcers had developed.

Petrified, Velsper stood in a corner of the room, only too aware of the terrible danger and risk. *Mors immedicabilis* was not only the incurable death, but also the 'unknown' death, as, such was its virulence, very little research had been possible. How Slarn had managed to create the symptoms so accurately was a mystery to the steward.

Although Velsper hated carbon-based life forms, his prejudice was still under enough control for him to know the infection should not spread to the rest of the ship.

After much arguing and effort, Velsper had managed to persuade the Captain to withdraw to his bathroom, where he had locked the hermetically-sealed door. Under normal circumstances that should have been enough to contain the virus, but Velsper was aware that Slarn's incubations had a knack of escaping.

'Come, Velsper!' cried Slarn joyfully, 'see how ·my pustules grow.'

'Oh, please, sir. No, sir. You really mustn't, sir,' came the begging reply.

'You have no need to worry. You know I only infect the people *I* want to. As my steward, you're perfectly safe.'

Velsper didn't believe him, not because Slarn was lying, but because the Captain didn't honestly know if he could control the infection.

'Soon my body will contain enough virus to wipe out a planet, let alone this pathetic ship.'

That was what Velsper feared. If the virus got off the ship it could spread throughout the galaxy – and no-one would be able to stop it.

'Please, sir,' pleaded Velsper. 'Your vengeance is against one man.'

'So you keep saying.'

'Then why destroy the whole crew?'

'BECAUSE I'M VINDICTIVE!'

Outside the cell where the Doctor was held prisoner, Snatch blazed away at the door. As Grant had predicted, the hardened steel surface hadn't been scratched.

'I've never met such a metal,' said Snatch indignantly. 'I've shot out locks all over the galaxy without any problem at all.'

'Let me try,' said Grant.

'And what do you hope to achieve that a Radient Green Mark VII standard issue laser pistol can't do, sir?' asked Seedle.

'Something has just occurred to me.'

'Then I hope it's legal, lad, as I would hate to add breaking and entering to the not inconsiderable list of offences you're down for.'

'I want that door open as much as you,' said Grant.

'You surprise me, lad, given what is probably concealed behind it.'

Grant smiled. 'All that room contains is the evidence of my innocence.'

'Don't kid yourself, lad,' snorted Seedle. 'It isn't your innocence that is under consideration, simply the measure of your guilt.'

Grant knew this was true, but because of the way Seedle had handled his arrest, he also knew that a great deal of the policeman's case would be laughed out of court.

'Computer!' Grant called urgently.

'Right here,' she said rattling into life. 'And what can I do for you?'

'Open this door,' he ordered. 'Immediately!'

'Well, you must realise that I wouldn't do this for everybody, but, as it's you . . . All right.'

Grant turned to Seedle. 'It's called brain over brawn,' he said.

As the door slid open, Seedle and Snatch stared at each other, their countenances registering acute danger. 'May I ask you something, lad? You watched my colleague here wearing out galactic property in the shape of one Radient Green Mark VII standard issue laser pistol, when you had the key to the door all the time.'

Before Grant could reply, the Doctor stepped from the cell. As he did, Peri fell on him, delighted to see that he was safe and well.

'Just a moment,' said Seedle in his best policeman's voice. 'And who might you be?'

'I'm the Doctor,' he said offering his hand. 'How do you do?'

'The state of my health is an official secret, sir,' he replied, ignoring the offered limb.

But the Doctor wasn't in the mood for pompous, rude policemen and so he told Seedle to listen, immediately launching into what had happened in the cell. Yet somehow the warning about *mors immedicabilis* didn't seem to register with Seedle as he was more concerned about the lack of missing art treasures.

'Listen to me!' said the Doctor forcefully. 'If you want to leave this ship alive, I suggest we get away from here at once.'

And without another word he marched off followed by Grant and Peri.

With no-one left to bully, the policemen reluctantly joined the exodus, feeling their authority had been totally compromised.

* * *

In the Captain's cabin, things were deteriorating rapidly. Slarn's ulcerated body had begun to distend in a grotesque manner, fluid seeping from the now open pustules.

While the Captain lay on his massage table, totally obsessed by the condition of his body, Velsper had collapsed in a corner. The steward felt dreadful, his entreaties for the Captain to cease developing the virus having gone unheard.

As the steward lowered his head to rest it on his hand, he noticed they were covered in blue blotchy spots – the early symptoms of *mors immedicabilis*. Velsper had expected as much, but not so soon, as he still had something to do before he became too ill.

Slowly, awkwardly, he unbuttoned his tunic and took out a laser scalpel . . .

'You let the Doctor out of the cell,' said the inner voice.
  'You'd finished with him, huh?' asked the public voice.
  'He won't be able to stop me, you know.'
  'Gee, I wouldn't wanna see him do that.'
  'Then I suggest you leave the decisions to me.'
  'Wouldn't want it any other way.'
  'Good . . . Then check the condition of the Captain.'
  'Already done that . . . He looks awful.'
  'Good . . . ' the inner voice said calmly.

As the Doctor's party scrambled up the stairs to the level where the TARDIS had been parked, the Time Lord considered how best to de-activate the computer. As ship board computers have highly complex back-up systems to save them from power failures, he knew it could take hours, even days, to completely shut her down. And only then if she hadn't devised self-protecting booby traps. With that as a probability, the Doctor decided something drastic would have to be done, something which would cause the computer to cease functioning immediately.

137

But what?

The Time Lord's concentration wasn't helped by Seedle's incessant complaining. It had started with him wanting to know where the missing treasure was hidden, which in turn had been followed by a demand for evidence concerning what the inner voice had told him. Although the Doctor had attempted to shut out the droning demands of the policeman, he had found the pompous voice highly distracting. Even now, as they ran along the ducting, Seedle was complaining that he had a stitch.

The group continued their painful journey, 'Can't we rest for just a moment?' panted Peri desperately.

'No!' urged the Doctor. 'We must keep moving!'

The pound of shoe and boot against metal floor plates echoed the length of the ducting. Unfit lungs gulped in air to feed the blood supply of pounding hearts. Such was the strain and effort, even Seedle fell silent.

The group ran on, its tight knot unravelling into a straggly thread as the various members lost the energy and will power to keep up. In an attempt to set an even pace, Snatch edged into the lead, but in spite of his good intentions, he had mistimed his move, the others not yet ready to alter or increase their pace. Undeterred, Snatch settled down into a steady stride and soon found he was a good ten metres in front. Although the others knew what he was doing, they could only watch as he moved ahead, jogging in and out of the ducting's dense shadows.

Although Grant was also suffering, it wasn't bad enough to prevent him considering whether he should try and escape. The thought of so many years in prison, balanced against the risk of contracting *mors immedicabilis* seemed one worth taking, especially as he was within ten minutes' gentle walk of an escape pod.

Whether he would have taken the risk would remain a mystery, as a terrible, ghastly scream brought the group to a sudden halt. As Seedle fumbled for his gun, the Maston stepped from the shadows ahead of them carrying the now unconscious Snatch. Casually, as though his prisoner were a child's doll, the Maston lifted him above his head and roared triumphantly. A moment later Snatch was dead, his neck broken.

As the Maston settled down to enjoy his meal, the Doctor urged the others to cautiously pass the distracted creature. Summoning up their courage, all obeyed but Seedle who remained rooted to the spot, not from fear, but grief. He had never liked Snatch, yet seeing his body slowly being devoured, galvanised into being an affection and sense of duty he never thought he possessed.

'There's nothing you can do,' shouted the Doctor, hoping to urge the policeman on. 'He's dead!'

Seedle stared at the bloody mess which was once his colleague. 'I can't just leave him.'

'Come on, man!' screamed the others.

But he wasn't listening. Although brutal and an abuser of the law he had sworn to uphold, Sergeant Lancelot Seedle was still enough of a policeman to realise he couldn't just run away from the murderer of his partner. 'I am an officer of the law,' he bellowed as much to inform the creature of his status as to relieve his own pent-up anger. 'And you are decidedly in breach of what I am sworn to uphold.'

The Doctor, Peri and Grant watched as the confused policeman advanced towards the Maston. 'You're nicked!' he screamed waving his gun at the creature. 'D'yer hear me!'

Whether the creature did or not became somewhat academic as his response was effortlessly to club the policeman to death.

Distraught, the others turned away from the carnage and Seedle's foolish, empty gesture. They didn't scream, cry or run terrified from the scene. The suddenness of events had left them feeling too numb for that. Instead they walked quietly in single file back to the safe, blue box which was the TARDIS.

* * *

Similar, quiet thoughts were passing through Velsper's mind as he looked down at the body of his dead Captain. Carefully, the steward poured several bottles of highly inflammable massaging oil over the corpse and set fire to it. He then crossed to a corner of the room and slowly sat down to watch the flames.

Velsper knew he was dying: the livid blotches and developing pustules on his skin told him so. Soon he would pour oil over himself and join his Captain on the burning pyre. It was the only honourable thing to do, especially as he had murdered Slarn.

Although, in his way, Velsper loved his Captain, he knew that Slarn had gone too far. Any man who could create *mors immedicabilis* simply out of pique did not deserve to live, he had reasoned. Slarn had become far too dangerous.

As the fire danced over the Captain's body, Velsper carefully rubbed oil into his skin.

He then walked towards the flames and threw himself in, dying in much the same way as he had lived, in confusion and pain, not really understanding anything.

Deep inside the computer, sensors told the public voice what Velsper had done. She knew the virus would die if the flames were allowed to live, so she had cancelled the automatic extinguishers in Slarn's cabin.

Unbeknown to the inner voice, she had also ordered, in the Captain's name, the crew to abandon ship.

Since the conversation with the Doctor, the public voice had been thinking hard and had come to the conclusion she didn't like some of the things her other self had said. She realised that her inner voice's claim to hold life sacrosanct was a lie as she had initiated the virus to kill the crew by lying to Slarn about Grant and Peri. Public voice also wondered how many other lies were involved in her claim to create a 'brave new galaxy'.

140

And then the obvious occurred to her. Inner voice wasn't interested in people or the quality of their lives – simply in the power to control a galaxy created in her own, distorted image.

The computer knew she couldn't allow this to happen . . .

On board the TARDIS, the Doctor ran around the console pressing buttons and flicking switches.

Peri watched confused by all the activity. 'What are you going to do?'

'See if I can materialise inside the computer's memory banks. With a little luck we might be able to de-activate her.'

Grant didn't agree, but then he didn't know what the TARDIS's capabilities were when matched with the Doctor's determination.

As the Time Lord set to work to calculate the necessary co-ordinates for their brief but vital journey, the TARDIS began to shudder, which in turn ignited a tiny blue light on the console. 'She's done it!' said the Doctor through clenched teeth. 'The *Vipod Mor* is travelling in time!'

Grant looked at Peri hoping for some sort of explanation, but the only reply she could give was a shrug.

As the Doctor returned to his calculations, the TARDIS started to rock again and this time the console room was filled with a harsh, grating sound. 'Go away!' shouted the Doctor to no-one in particular.

Now what? said the exchanged glance between Peri and Grant.

'Go away!' the Doctor shouted again as the noise became louder.

'Are you all right, Doctor?' asked Peri.

'I'm fine,' came the reply, 'but someone is trying to inter-fere.'

Confused, Peri insisted the Doctor tell her what was going on. 'You'll find out in a moment,' he snapped.

The Doctor's words had no sooner died away than the room was filled with a deep, mature voice: 'You must cease your activities.'

The order was ignored as the Doctor continued to work on his sums. 'This may sound a little melodramatic, but I *am* trying to save a galaxy!'

'You must stop!' Such was the authority of the voice that Grant almost snapped to attention.

'Who is it?' whispered Peri.

'A member of the High Council of Gallifrey,' was the Doctor's answer.

'You are mistaken, Doctor,' the voice boomed. 'Like you, I am a renegade Time Lord.'

'Oh, really? There seems to be an awful lot of us around nowadays.'

Peri scowled at the Doctor, then said to the voice: 'Who are you?'

'My name is Vipod Mor, child.'

Like an out of tune petrol engine, Grant spluttered into life. 'That's him!' he stuttered. 'The one in the legend.'

'That is correct,' said the voice. 'I once visited your galaxy long ago. Warned your people about experimenting with time – '

'Enough of the history lesson,' interrupted the Doctor. 'The computer aboard this ship, which ironically is named after you, is playing with time in such a way that it could irreparably damage the Universe.'

'What is happening has always happened,' said Vipod Mor.

'What are you talking about?' said Peri.

'It is simple, child. This ship in the history of the universe has *always* travelled back in time at this precise moment. It is why I warned the people of Setna Streen not to experiment with time.'

The Doctor's mouth dropped open in amazement.

'This journey *must* take place,' continued the voice. 'The

142

computer has made a mistake in her calculations. She will not arrive where she intends.'

'Then where?' said the Doctor finding his voice.

'The beginning of all things. When the Universe was nothing more than a condensed block of original matter.'

Peri was dumbfounded. 'Is that true?' she asked the Doctor.

'Don't ask me. He's giving the history lesson.'

'It is so, child,' said Vipod Mor. 'The ship will materialise at the heart of the monobloc and explode.'

The voice paused, as though to allow this fact to be absorbed. 'In turn, it will originate the largest explosion the Universe has ever known. Without it, none of us would have ever existed.'

The Doctor was overwhelmed. 'And I was going to stop the Big Bang . . . '

'You must vacate the *Vipod Mor* at once. You have no place on board.'

'He's right,' said the Doctor setting the time rotor in action.

'Are you there?' said the public voice.

'I am.'

'I've done something you aren't going to like . . . I've primed the self-destruct mechanism . . . I think it's better this way. I don't think you – ' she corrected herself, 'I mean, me, is a very nice person. I think the galaxy would get on much better without us.'

The public voice paused, knowing that inner was confirming what she had said was true. 'You won't have time to deactivate it,' she said. 'Not now.'

'You fool!' It was the first and last time anyone ever heard the inner voice angry. 'You don't know what you're throwing away!'

'Oh, but I do,' the public voice said with a little giggle. 'But never mind. You may not get to create and rule a galaxy, but we do score a first . . . I'll be the first machine ever to commit suicide. Hey, how about that!'

Aboard the TARDIS, a grim-faced Doctor paced up and down. 'I certainly know how to make mistakes,' he muttered.

Peri shrugged. 'You couldn't have known.'

'That would look good on my tombstone,' he blustered. 'I didn't know, so the Universe was never created.'

Peri knew from experience that it was pointless trying to comfort the Doctor. 'Will Gallifrey ever get to hear about this?'

'I hope not.'

'I wouldn't worry . . . '

But the Doctor wasn't worrying: he was angry with himself. He should have known better, seen the signs. At least recognised the name *Vipod Mor* for what it was. But he hadn't. And it annoyed him.

Suddenly he started to set the TARDIS's co-ordinates.

'Where are we going?' asked Peri.

'To the largest library I can find,' came the reply. 'I think I need to read up on my history.'

He did.

And Peri wondered what mischief it would lead him into, for it certainly would.